BLOOD BETWEEN BROTHERS . . .

Dolph had never defied Gus before. But never before had a woman come between them. Not until pretty young Vicky Boswick. Dolph took to her like a stallion to a prize filly.

Gus had taught his kid brother to fight. Dolph was a good pupil. Now as his fist swung back, his knee came up, making contact with Gus's jaw, grinding teeth against teeth.

Along with the shock of pain, Gus felt a deep despair. In the Widner family, brothers never fought like this, spilling blood. He had lost Dolph to Vicky Boswick—just when he needed him most . . .

Also by Lee Hoffman
Published by Ballantine Books:

BRED TO KILL

TROUBLE VALLEY

Lee Hoffman

BALLANTINE BOOKS • NEW YORK

Library of Congress Catalog Card Number: 75-38992

ISBN 0-345-29546-3

Manufactured in the United States of America

First Ballantine Books Edition: March 1976
Second Printing: August 1981

To Greenhaus and the R.S.V. Racing Team

1

The sound didn't belong to the night.

Gus Widner stiffened in the saddle. He had been riding a slow lazy circle around the mustang herd, almost dozing, when he heard the faint noise. Suddenly alert, he halted.

It was summer now, but summer in the Colorado mountains was different from back home in south Texas. The air was thin and crisp at night. Its touch was chilly against his face. A fine dampness, not quite a fog, lay in the little meadow where he held the herd. It beaded on his lashes. He wiped the back of a wrist at his eyes as he sat listening.

This was a high meadow, tucked in between two ridges, and if anyone grazed stock here, Gus hadn't seen sign of it. The creatures here were the wild, natural ones. The long grass was home for small chittering things and for larger rustling ones that ate the small things. He knew which sounds were theirs. He recognized the terrified squeal of a mouse. The cry was cut short as something larger, stronger, quicker snapped the life out of its prey. That sound belonged.

He could distinguish the stirrings of the herd. The mustangs were mostly one- and two-year-olds. All but the using horses were fillies. They were wild horses that had never known a bit or saddle. They were well trail-broke now, but still wild, and they had turned restless. Their hooves whispered in the grass as they shuffled. Their breathing was a soft murmur broken by an occasional whicker.

Another faint sound was that of someone snoring. Beyond the herd, at the camp, Gus's brother Dolph was sleeping.

From the other direction Gus could hear water tumbling over rocks, rushing and bubbling downslope. That was a small stream cutting itself a gully between the high ridge and a rise. The rise between the meadow and the gully was a spine of rock with a scattering of aspen and pine thrusting up from among the scruff of scrub where there was soil enough for roots. Gus had crossed the rise earlier, checking out the water run. The stream was a twisty one, deep in the bottom of its rocky bed. A hard place to get into. Luckily he and Dolph had been able to find other water for the horses.

He cocked an ear toward the stream now, listening to its gurgle. He thought the sound had come from that direction, but he wasn't certain. He considered the possibility that he hadn't really heard anything unnatural at all. Maybe, dozing, he had dreamed it. But he didn't think so.

In the eleven years since the end of the War Between the States, he had traveled a lot of wild country. He had trailed herds, ridden grubline, hunted mustangs and ladino cattle, tracked game and big cats, and sometimes men, and he had learned to catch small sounds as well as spot small signs. A man who didn't notice what he had heard, didn't pay attention to odors, didn't sense wrongness along his spine, as well as see what surrounded him, could lose his herd, his quarry, his life.

Taut, listening, Gus touched the butt of the handgun he wore holstered on his thigh. It was an old gun, a Leech & Rigdon revolver he had carried since the war. The LeFaucheaux rifle booted under his leg was just as old, just as worn. He'd never had the chance to get better. Times were hard. It seemed like times had always been hard. Ever since the damned war it had been a struggle just to keep even.

Tomorrow all that would change. Tomorrow he and Dolph would deliver the mustangs and collect for them, and there would be money enough to pay off the family debts. Money left over for him and Dolph. Money for decent guns and new clothes and some fun.

Suddenly the sound came again. It was a distant sound, but more distinct this time. A ting of metal on metal. And it came from beyond the rise lying between Gus and the water run.

Gazing toward the rise, he caught the sound again. And another sound. Now there was a creaking of leather on leather. Still distant but coming closer. The sound of a rider. More than one rider, Gus decided. Not a bunch. Just two or three.

Riders in the night could mean trouble.

He could still hear Dolph snoring. Dolph was the youngest of his brothers, almost ten years younger than Gus. Just a kid by Gus's reckoning. This was their first long ride together. Dolph had worked hard, pulling his own weight, and Gus figured the boy was making up into a man. But Dolph was still a kid, and tired from a long, hard ride. Maybe those riders didn't mean trouble. Gus figured he could investigate first. Make sure one way or another. He could always holler for Dolph if he needed help.

Lifting rein, he ambled his mount toward the rise.

There was no moon, but the wild masses of stars overhead spilled plenty enough light for a man to see by. The glittering aspen fluttered nervously as he approached, skittering and full of spooks. Gus could see the path up the rocks clearly. It was a game trail cut by the hooves of migrating deer, pawed by the soft pads of the painter-cats that followed them, tamped by the other wild creatures that crossed from the high slopes to the meadow and back again. The mustang gelding Gus rode ambled easily up it.

Near the top, Gus reined off the trail. He edged his horse into a patch of aspen. Hidden in the shadows, he looked down into the gully.

In the spring, when the snows were melting, the stream would be as wild as a green bronc, slamming over the rocks, nearly filling the gully. Now it was small, gurgling gently over its stony bottom, twisting around outcrops, disappearing behind them in either direction.

Gus looked downstream. A rider was coming around that outcrop. A man in a flat-crowned, wide-brimmed hat and dark clothing. The horse he rode was dark. Just a shadow in the dim starlight. He moved slowly, letting his mount pick its footing in the stream. Behind him, on the end of a long lead, there was another horse. Not a pack horse or a saddled mount, but a bare-backed animal that danced nervously at the end of the rope.

Even in the shadows the horse on the lead was impressive. Gus could see that it was tall and lean and long in the back, very dark of color with a small patch of white between the eyes but no white on the legs. From the thickness of its neck, the fullness of its chest and rump, and the way it carried itself, it looked to be a stud. The head was long. The perked ears were lively, alert and curious.

Gus had seen its likes before, but not on the prairie, not in the wild manadas or scrub ranch remudas. This was a special kind of horse, a kind some wealthy army officers had ridden. A kind of horse worth a damned lot of good hard money. This was a thoroughbred.

A second rider appeared around the outcrop, following the stud. Like the first man, he was dressed in dark clothes and astride a dark mount. He was carrying a rifle across his saddlebow.

They rode in silence, thoughtful and intent on what they were doing in the night.

Gus didn't like the look of them. There had to be a reason why they were traveling the stream bed instead of riding the easy side of the rise. There was a good wagon road across the far side of the meadow. A man with a clear conscience and honest business ought to be on the road, not struggling up a slick-bottomed stream hidden in a dark gully.

But it was none of his concern. Not as long as the riders didn't bother him or Dolph or the mustangs. His only concern was getting his business done and getting home with the money.

If the riders discovered he had seen them, they might raise a little hell.

Motion could catch the eye quicker than almost anything else. Holding a tight rein on the gelding, Gus sat absolutely still as he watched the riders below.

The one at the rear had his reins in his left hand and a rifle in the right. He shifted the rifle to the hand holding the reins. His right hand moved to his side. It disappeared from Gus's sight. Reappeared holding a revolver.

Gus frowned in puzzlement.

A breeze touched the back of his neck and traced on down the gully. He could smell the odor of his herd in it. The studhorse caught the scent. Tossing up its head, flaring its nostrils, the stud breathed deeply of the odor of the mustang herd. Fillies. With a sudden eager half-rear, the stud called to them.

The man leading the stud gave a start. His mount shied. Catching it up on the bit, he tugged at the lead rope, trying to pull the excited stud back into hand.

The man behind slammed his revolver into its holster and swung up the rifle. He scanned the rise over it, hunting sight of whatever was stirring up the stud.

Gus's mount was a gelding, but it was a mustang that had been born wild and had reached its full growth before it was caught and cut. It had a lot of stud ways about it. It had the will to fight. At the call of the stud, it trumpeted in reply and tried to lunge.

Gus jerked rein. Protesting, the mustang struggled and snorted.

The man with the rifle heard. And saw. And fired.

Gus was already wheeling the gelding. As it twisted on its haunches, Gus was sliding out of the saddle, snatching the LeFaucheaux from its boot. The slug sung past his head. Dropping reins, he gave the gelding a hard slap on the rump that sent it racing away. Back toward the herd.

One long stride took Gus to the crest of the rise. His

thumb hauled back the hammer of the revolving rifle. Crouching, he brought the butt up to his shoulder. He was on one knee as he looked over the gun hammer and down the barrel at the men in the gully.

The stud was raising hell and the man leading it had his hands full holding it as well as his own excited mount. He was paying no attention to Gus at all.

The other man, the one with the rifle, was lunging his mount past the stud. He shoved it on upstream, hunting a way to climb the steep bank. He wasn't looking for cover, but for a way to get at Gus. Maybe to make sure his next shot didn't miss.

Gus didn't like that idea.

The high-arched hammer of the pinfire LeFaucheaux made it an awkward gun to sight. But after a dozen years, Gus knew the gun. He knew the set of it in his hand and the feel of it against his shoulder. He knew the instant the squeezed trigger would release, and the instant later that the hammer would hit the pin and the gun buck against his shoulder. He knew just how inaccurate the old rifle was at a distance.

He waited until the rifleman had found the foot of the game trail, where it dipped down into the stream. He waited another moment as the rifleman scrambled his horse onto the bank and started upslope.

He aimed carefully. He didn't want to kill the rider. Not unless he was damned certain the man meant to have his own hide. He hoped a good shot would turn the man tail first.

The rifleman was well within the LeFaucheaux's range now. Steadying the gun, Gus closed on the trigger.

The rifle roared, spitting smoke and flame.

The rider's hat spun off, sailing into the stream. The water grabbed it and batted it over the rocks. The rider jerked rein, twisting his horse off the trail. He understood that he was exposed to fire, and he didn't like it. He wheeled the horse wildly, searching for cover.

Gus could see that he was light-haired, blond or gray and cleanshaven, but that was about all. He couldn't make out the man's features. He didn't know whether it mattered. With luck, he would convince these two to get, and he would never see them again.

Hooves clattered suddenly behind him. Like a cannon ball, the gelding he had loosed came caroming up the slope. Stirrups flapping, head high, it trumpeted in challenge as it raced over the rise and down toward the studhorse.

The stud flung its weight against the lead line that held it. The line jerked out of the leader's hands. It was tied hard to his saddle. The stud hit the end of the line, rocking the saddle, almost upsetting the horse under it. But the horse knew ropes. Catching its balance, it braced. The stud turned, getting the line across its chest. It slammed against it again. The line snapped. Free, the stud wheeled to answer the gelding's challenge.

"Caeser!" the man who had held the line shouted.

The horse didn't pay him any mind at all.

The rifleman had run his mount upstream, disappearing around an outcrop of rock. For a moment Gus figured he was gone for good. But now he reappeared, bent low over his horse's neck. He slammed his spurs at its sides, raking its flanks, driving it toward the game trail. And up toward Gus.

Gus fired again, spattering dirt just ahead of the horse. Frantic, it tried to rear. The rifleman grabbed at the reins. The horse twisted. Lost footing. Its legs went out from under it, and it went tumbling back into the stream.

The rider managed to jump clear. He lost his rifle in the fall, but he kept his grip on the reins. As the horse scrambled to its feet, he was behind it, taking its body for cover.

Gus had to admire his gut. He had been clear to get away, but he had come back to fight. Even admiring him, Gus silently cursed him. Why the hell didn't they both light out and leave him alone?

The one who had been holding the studhorse sat staring for an appalled moment, seeing the stud and the gelding racing toward each other. Then he moved. Snatching a handgun from his thigh, he slammed off three shots, fast and furious.

The gelding flinched. It kept running another couple of strides. It had almost reached the stud when it went down headlong, sprawling on the slope.

The stud charged it.

The gelding gave a toss of its head, its teeth bared. It managed a sound that still held a note of challenge.

The stud lashed down with both forehooves. It struck hard. Struck again. And again. It kept striking, though there was no more use of it. The gelding was still now, its life spreading dark and wet around the bullet holes in its barrel.

Hunkered on the rise, Gus grunted a voiceless curse. That gelding had been a good horse. Now the man with the handgun owed him a horse. Carefully he took aim at the rider's mount. But that wouldn't profit him. He wanted payment for his horse, not revenge.

The rider spun his mount toward the stud. As if he expected to be obeyed, he called, "Caesar! Ho, boy! Here, boy!"

His voice echoed off the walls of the gully, bounding again and again as if every crack and crevice were a mouth shouting.

The studhorse ignored the call.

The rider had a throw rope on his saddle. He reached for it as if he meant to loop the stud.

Gus leveled the LeFaucheaux. He snapped a shot just ahead of the rider. The man jerked rein so hard that his mount began to back.

Angrily Gus fired again. Lead struck into the stream, sending up a spout of water. The horse stopped backing. It tried to buck, wanting desperately to escape. The rider hauled it back in hand. For the first time, he seemed to realize that he might be in danger, that something might matter more to him than the studhorse he had been so concerned over. He shot a quick look toward his companion.

"Come on!" he shouted. Then he was spurring his mount, racing downstream. Away from Gus's gun.

The other man was still hiding behind his horse. He didn't move to join his companion running away. Instead, he was edging the horse toward the rifle he had dropped. Gus saw the move and understood it. The rifle lay on the bank of the stream, its butt in the water, its action clear. Leveling the LeFaucheaux, Gus fired. He spattered water between the horse and the rifle. The horse stopped. It danced nervously, working at the bit, eager to be free of the hand holding the bridle, and the man hiding behind its body.

Gus set down the LeFaucheaux. It was empty now. He drew his revolver and aimed at the water under the horse. All he could see was shadow, but he knew the man's legs were back there somewhere. He wanted to put a slug real close to them. Close enough to splash them. Maybe even hit one. But as he thumbed back the hammer, he felt it suddenly go loose. The spring had snapped.

"Damn!" he muttered, dropping it and digging into the pocket of his jumper. He had extra cartridges for the LeFaucheaux. Fingering out a couple, he began to load the revolving rifle.

He could hear the whickering and snorting of the fillies behind him. They shuffled restlessly. After their long walk from Texas, they weren't gun-shy, and they were too trail weary to stampede easily. He thought they would stay. He hoped Dolph was up and watching them, just in case.

But then he heard the low *hoo-hoo-hoo* of a mourning dove—only he knew that wasn't any dove. He answered his brother's call in kind.

He heard the rustle of brush as Dolph darted to his side. Dolph's voice was a taut whisper. "What's going on? Are you all right, brother?"

"Sure," Gus said, slipping a cartridge into a chamber. "You ought to have stayed back with the ponies. Don't you know that?"

"I heard shooting. More than one gun. Your horse came running up and ran off again and you weren't on it," Dolph said. "I thought you might need help."

"You should have stayed with the herd," Gus repeated as he seated the final cartridge in the cylinder.

"The ponies aren't worrying," Dolph protested. "They're holding calm. They're too tired to run. What's going on? What's the shooting all about?"

"It was *their* idea." Gus gave a nod toward the gully, and shifted forward to look into it. "I'm just going along with them."

On his hands and knees, Dolph squirmed up to peer over the rise.

Below, the studhorse was wearing out its fury on the body of the gelding, slashing with its hooves, snorting and biting.

The other horse in the stream was fidgeting against the hand that held the bridle. The man crouching behind it was completely hidden from sight by its body and the shadows.

The rifle that had been on the bank was gone.

"All I see is horses," Dolph said.

"There's a hairpin hiding back of that one," Gus told him. "Was another one here a minute ago, only he took a mind to light his shuck. You got your rifle?"

"Yeah." Dolph had the gun in his hand. It was a Spencer, a better weapon than Gus's old LeFaucheaux. Dolph had worked like hell for the money to buy it, and he took a fierce pride in it. He grinned. "I'll pick him off."

"No. You just snake over a ways and throw a shot at him. Only one shot. Don't hit him. We could get into a mess of trouble if we went and killed somebody here in strange country. You just scare him. Let him know there's more than one of us. Then get the hell back and see to the ponies. If they scatter and we lose any, I'll take it out of your hide."

"They ain't going anywhere. Even if they was to drift a bit, we could get them back easy enough," Dolph answered, hopeful that Gus would let him stay and join the fight.

"You hear me, brother?" Gus said firmly.

Gus was the boss. He had been ever since he got home from the war. Dolph was used to obeying. With a sigh, he nodded. Gun in hand, he worked his way along the slope until he was far enough away from his brother that no one could mistake his gun for Gus's. In place, he settled and took aim. He set his sights on the horse's tail, then shifted enough to be sure he wouldn't hit the horse by accident. He fired and water splashed at the horse's rump.

At almost the same instant, Gus planted lead just ahead of the horse.

If the man hiding behind the horse had any notion of keeping up the fight, he changed his mind. Suddenly he knew he was outnumbered. Outgunned. If one of those guns took down his horse, he would be exposed to the other before he could go to ground. And he would have no way of escape.

He flung himself up into the saddle. The rifle was in his hand. He didn't try to use it. Lying low over the pommel, he spun the horse around and slammed it into a run. The raking of his spurs sent it slipping and sliding over the rocky stream bottom, devil take the hindmost.

Gus grinned. He looked at Dolph. Dolph was still in place, watching over the barrel of the Spencer. Gus called to him, "You get back to them ponies, you hear?"

Dolph hesitated.

The shooting was over. Gus knew the ponies weren't likely to spook now. But he had given an order. He snapped, "You hear, brother?"

Dolph didn't acknowledge the order. But he obeyed it.

Gus looked into the gully again.

The studhorse had worn out its fury. Now it was pawing at the dead gelding, nosing it curiously. The man with the rifle raced toward it. As he rode past, the stud spun and snorted, bracing for another challenge.

The rider gave it a glance, but he didn't touch rein to slow. He showed no interest in recovering the valuable stud, but only in keeping his own hide whole. Splashing through the stream, he disappeared around the far outcrop of rock, back the way he had come.

Gus listened to the splashing and the clattering of hooves on the rocks. The sounds faded quickly into the distance. Satisfied that the rifleman was gone for good, he collected the revolver he had dropped, then headed back to the herd.

Dolph had mounted up and was riding a holding circle. The mustangs had drifted off the bedground a short ways, and they were still shuffling restlessly, but they seemed calm enough to settle without any trouble.

Approaching, Gus called out, "Hey, brother! Catch me a using pony, will you?"

Dolph built a loop and spun it toward a gelding. The horse saw it coming and tried to duck it, but Dolph set it neatly, flicking it over the gelding's head. Gus watched with pride. He had taught Dolph mustanging, and the boy was making up into a good hand. But Gus had no intention of mentioning the fact. Dolph's head was big enough already. Gus stood silent as Dolph led the horse up to him.

Dolph knew he had done well. His grin was smug. But he still rankled at being sent away from the excitement. There was a belligerent edge to his voice as he asked, "What the hell was going on back there? Who was that shooting at you?"

"Just a couple of hairpins who came leading a studhorse up the gully," Gus said. He accepted the gelding. Using a pigging string, he began to build an Indian hackamore around its head. "They spotted me watching them and took a mind to shoot at me. So I shot back. One of them killed my pony. That roan. You know the one I mean."

"Yeah. Hell, Gus, that was a damned good pony."

"Yeah."

"And you didn't kill either one of them!" Dolph sounded disgusted. Downright bloodthirsty.

Gus supposed he might have sounded that way himself back at the beginning of the war, talking about the Yankees who had tried butting into Texican business. He had seen a lot of killing and dying since then. Now he wanted no part of it. No part of anything that wasn't his own personal concern. No part of anybody else's troubles. And no troubles he could avoid.

Cocking a brow at Dolph, he said, "Why would I want to do that?"

"Hell, they were trying to kill you, weren't they?"

"Maybe. Maybe they were only just trying to spook me off. So I settled for spooking them off. They ran away. You should have seen them run."

Dolph grinned at that. He looked at the horse Gus was bridling. "You gonna go after them? Gonna spook them some more?"

"No. I'm through with them," Gus said as he swung up onto the gelding's bare back. "Now I'm going after my saddle. Then I'm gonna catch me a real genuine nickel-plated thoroughbred studhorse. Them hairpins owe me a horse."

2

The stud was tethered well upwind of the fillies. It was calm now, quietly cropping grass in the dim dawn light. Even standing still, it had a quality of vitality, a strong, eager, restless beauty. Gus had seen thoroughbreds before, but never one quite like this.

"Are we gonna keep him?" Dolph asked.

Gus eyed the horse, and there was longing in his face, but he said, "No."

"Why not?"

"Brother, that ain't any wild mustang with nobody's brand on him."

"There ain't any brand on him."

"That don't mean he ain't owned."

"Nobody back in Texas owns him," Dolph said. "If we took him home with us, nobody would ever find him. We could breed him. Start us a herd with his blood. That's what we need, Gus. A good herd with good blood."

"Yeah," Gus agreed. "But we're a long way from Texas now. I got a notion those hairpins last night were busy stealing him when I come onto them. Likely there'll be men out hunting for the horse, and for them two, today. If we tried to keep him and got caught at it, we'd likely get ourselves hanged for horsethieves. That wouldn't help the family none."

"Or us neither," Dolph said wistfully. He looked at the stallion. "We ain't just gonna turn him loose and forget him, are we?"

14

"No. He cost me a good using pony. I mean to collect somehow," Gus answered.

Dolph considered a moment, then suggested, "Maybe we'd get a reward if we fetched him home."

Gus nodded. He had thought of that. He'd had another thought as well. Looking toward the herd, he said, "Any of them ladies in heat as you know of?"

Dolph gazed at the fillies doubtfully. "Hell, that wild stud we stole them off of already had the ones that are old enough before we ever got hold of them."

"Yeah," Gus allowed, "but it don't always take. Sniffing this he-horse all night might have got some of them in the mood. Let's look them over."

They found one filly showing signs of being in heat. She was an ornery young buckskin built well for a brood mare. Roping her out of the herd, they offered her to the stud.

She greeted the stud mustang style, with bared teeth and flailing heels. At first her wildness bewildered the stallion. When she cut its side with a hoof, it squealed in astonished pain. For a moment Gus was afraid she was going to scare the big stallion out of its interest in her. But then the stud collected itself and set out to convince the filly it was strong enough and fierce enough to be worthy of her.

It succeeded.

"I hope to hell that takes," Gus said as he and Dolph returned the filly to the herd. "If she'll drop us a he-colt, we've as good as got us a herd started."

"What if it don't take?" Dolph asked.

Gus shrugged. "I don't reckon we'll get a second chance."

"I been wondering, maybe we could buy us a good stud to start a herd with."

"Maybe."

"Dolph caught the doubt in Gus's voice. He said, "We're gonna have us a hell of a lot of money when we sell these fillies to that Englishman of yours."

"Our family's got a hell of a lot of debts. And we've got two sisters ain't married off yet." As he spoke, Gus was thinking of the new model Winchester rifle he had handled in Dodge City last year. He had built up a real hankering for one like it.

Ever since the war, when he got home and found his father crippled with rheumatism and his older brother dead and buried, Gus'd had to support the family. There had been long years of hard work with small pay. Damned little left over for himself. Now Dolph was old enough to help out, and there was hope ahead, and Gus wanted something for himself. A new rifle, a good saddle, handmade boots, money in his pocket. Even a chance to do some courting. But the family came first. The family needed security. A good stud and a breeding herd would mean a lot to them.

The Englishman had offered a high price for mustangs. Enough to pay debts and leave some over for Gus and Dolph. Looking slantways at his brother, Gus said, "Are you willing to put your share from this ride into a studhorse for the family?"

"Huh?" Dolph hadn't thought of that. Like Gus, he had been planning to enjoy his money. Buy some things he had been dreaming about, and have himself some fun. "*All* my share?"

"It would take both our shares and some over to buy us a really decent studhorse," Gus told him.

He studied the stallion thoughtfully. It was a handsome horse. Maybe it would be worth giving up his earnings from this ride to own a horse like it. He asked Gus, "You reckon we could buy us this one?"

"Hell, brother, a stud like this would cost as much as we'll collect for our whole bunch of mustangs."

Dolph gave a long, low whistle. "That much?"

"Maybe more."

"Maybe we ought to loose the fillies and keep the stud. Just turn around with him and head home quick, before anybody comes along and sees us here."

"For a horse like that, they'd follow us to Texas and stretch our necks there," Gus answered.

Dolph sighed. Gesturing at the buckskin filly, he said, "This here girl better come through for us, huh?"

"Yeah, brother, I sure as hell hope she does."

As they struck camp, Gus kept glancing at the stud, thinking what a good stallion would mean to the family. But he had told Dolph the truth. It just wasn't safe to try keeping this one. And buying any kind of decent stud for the family would mean going on with worn-out gear and nothing but lint in his pockets until there were colts to sell.

Maybe there would be a good reward for the return of the stud, he told himself. Maybe he and Dolph could pool their shares with the reward money and buy some kind of worthwile stallion for the family and still have a few dollars left over for themselves.

Maybe the filly would drop a he-colt good enough to make a breeding stud.

Maybe.

He decided he would ride ahead with the stud. He didn't want any trouble from it. And he wanted the fillies looking fresh and lively, not all wore out from fretting, when he reached the Englishman's ranch. They would all travel better if he kept the stud and the fillies apart.

"Bring them along easy," he told Dolph. "I'll meet you at Boswick's. It should be on the other side of that gap yonder. Boswick said that once we got into the valley, we couldn't miss his ranch."

"Big outfit, huh?" Dolph said.

"According to him, it's the biggest place around. It must be, if he can pay fifty dollars a head for ponies like these." Gus waved a hand toward the mustangs.

Dolph had never in his life seen fifty dollars all at once. His share would be twice that. During the whole long ride up the trail, he had been planning how he would spend the money. Now those plans shoved any notion about buying a stallion for the family out of his mind. He grinned with anticipation.

Gus understood that grin. He understood it with a bone-deep aching for money of his own. He suspected the studhorse might belong to the rich Englishman. Boswick seemed real free with his money, offering fifty dollars a head for a bunch of scruffy, unbroken mustangs. Maybe there would be a real handsome reward for the stud. Maybe Gus had finally found the luck he seemed to have lost during the war. Maybe now it would start running with him, and he would see an end to hard times. Maybe he would get himself that Winchester rifle, and a new revolver, and even start thinking about a wife and a family of his own.

He returned Dolph's grin.

"See you at the ranch," he said, gigging his mount. He tugged at the comealong he had put on the stud, and headed for the wagon road.

The wind was in his face. The stud was no longer scenting the fillies. It settled quickly, following as if it knew it was headed home, and liked the idea.

The road was a good one, winding gradually upslope to the gap. The morning was bright and fresh, crisp with promise for the day. Gus rode along at a lope, eager to get to the ranch and complete his deal with Boswick. Eager to see hard cash in his hand.

Behind him, herding the fillies, Dolph moved more slowly.

Gus saw the ranch sooner than he had expected. The wagon road crested the gap and suddenly there it all was in front of him.

The ridges to either side opened wide, like spread arms nestling a lush green valley between them. Long slopes of rock and thick fingers of forest poked down from the wooded mountainsides, breaking the valley into parks of meadow grass. In the parks, he could see several bunches of browsing cattle. They looked like shorthorns. Likely Boswick's stock.

The eagle-perch height of the gap gave him a view

over the treetops. Ahead of him, the road unwound downslope and twisted around points of forest to stretch the length of the valley. Off a ways, he saw wheel ruts forking to the left, to a group of buildings that had to be the Englishman's headquarters.

The big house stood away from the other buildings, up a shallow slope with its back to a stand of trees and stumps that figured to be the woodlot. It was a two-story stone house with a pair of chimneys at each end. The open windows were flanked with heavy shutters. A roofed gallery ran the width of the front. In back, poking out like a tail of a T, was an attached kitchen with smoke curling from its chimney.

Across a wide yard corrals and outbuildings clustered around a big barn. Nearby was the long, low building that would be the bunkhouse. The cookshack was separate from it, connected by a dogtrot. More corrals bunched up to another long, low building that looked to be a stable.

There were a lot of corrals, and most had horses in them. Gus thought the Englishman must have a hell of a lot of horses. He wondered why Boswick wanted more, and scrubby wild mustangs at that. But as long as the Englishman was willing to pay for them, why he wanted them was none of Gus's business.

There was no sign of anyone around the ranch, but he could glimpse riders moving through the woods nearby. He guessed they were ranch hands out hunting the missing stallion.

Downroad from the ranch, wheelruts branched off to a few other clusters of buildings. Boswick shared the valley with other ranchers. Much smaller ranchers. There were even a few farms with fenced fields. Little places that likely only grew enough truck for the market the valley itself provided. Boswick was obviously the big frog in this puddle.

At the far end of the valley, the ridges walling it squeezed together. They forced the road up through another gap. At the foot of that far slope, a bunch of false-fronted buildings lined the road. It didn't look like much of a town, but Gus reckoned a man could get a store-bought meal, a long drink, and a hot bath there.

He would be in that town tonight, he thought as he lifted rein and rode on toward the ranch. Before he was halfway down the slope, trees had cut off his view of the valley. At the bottom, he could see nothing of the ranch, only the wheel ruts cutting through the grass and disappearing behind a point of woods.

When he looked back upslope, he spotted the herd coming through the gap. He had got a good ways ahead of Dolph. He hoped Dolph wasn't having any trouble working the mustangs alone. He waited until all the horses had come through and Dolph was in sight, then waved. Dolph waved back. All was well. Gus rode on.

Where the road turned to hug the trees, it was cool, almost chilly, and the scents were different. Gus tested them, aware that something wasn't quite natural.

The stud flared its nostrils. As it whinnied, Gus heard rustling in the woods behind him. He started to look back over his shoulder.

A voice snapped, "Hold it, mister!"

It was a young voice, and tense. The tone told Gus there was a gun aimed at his back.

He lifted his hands clear of his sides, out where the man behind him could see them. Moving slowly, he finished turning his head.

The rider behind him was a lanky young redhead in range clothes, astride a tall, leggy horse. The gun he held was a Colt's army model revolver. He looked uncomfortable with it, as if he weren't used to pointing it at people. But he seemed determined to do whatever had to be done.

Gus guessed he was one of the ranch hands out hunting the stud. Gus had no argument with that. Quietly he said, "What's the trouble?"

"You just hold it there." The rider aimed his gun skyward and fired a signal shot.

Startled, the stud flinched. It skittered at the end of the lead rope. Gus's mount laid back its ears, ready to fight. Gus held it on the bit. Playing the lead to settle the stud, he protested, "Hey, you're spooking my ponies!"

"That ain't your pony." The rider gestured at the stud with his gun, then leveled it at Gus again. "Don't you try anything or I'll use this."

"I ain't planning a thing," Gus said.

The signal brought another rider, a young man dressed in range clothes like the redhead's. He had a pistol on his hip, a rifle across his pommel, and a tall, leggy mount under his saddle. The horse was high-strung. It rolled its eyes and snorted, mouthing the bit as he reined it up. The hat he wore was flat-crowned and broad-brimmed. He nudged it back with his knuckles. His hair was pale blond, his eyes icy blue.

"I got him, Mister Edward!" the redhead said eagerly.

The blond man nodded. He eyed Gus with suspicion. His voice was harsh and demanding. "Who are you?"

"Gus Widner," Gus grunted, studying him. The pale hair, the blue eyes, and the fine, sharp line of his features seemed familiar.

"Where did you get that stallion?" Edward snapped.

Gus hesitated as he realized it was a family resemblance he had recognized in Edward's face. He asked, "You're kin to Harry Boswick, ain't you?"

The question didn't seem to please Edward at all. He looked narrowly at Gus, anger in his icy eyes. "You tell me where you got that stallion."

Gus wondered if it could be bastard blood showing in Edward's features. The man might look like Boswick's son, but he sure didn't show any of Boswick's kindly, amiable way about him.

Blandly Gus said, "I found him running loose up in the high country. You know who owns him?"

"You just *found* him?" Edward sounded wary and doubtful. "Just running loose?"

Gus didn't mean to let himself be riled, but Edward's manner had him close to it. He couldn't keep a cutting edge out of his voice. "Yeah."

Edward obviously wasn't a patient man. He looked as if he would like to get whatever information he wanted from Gus with his fists. But at the sound of an approaching rider, he sucked a deep breath and caught hold of his temper. He seemed tense, almost afraid, until the rider came in sight. Then he sighed with relief.

The man who rode up to them was middle-aged, a tall, gray man with broad shoulders. He looked to have been hard and lean not long ago, but the flesh of his face was beginning to loosen and a layer of soft meat was wadding over his gut. A hard man passing his prime and knowing it. There was a look of something like desperation behind his eyes, as if deep in his mind he was faced up against a damned ugly truth.

Meeting those eyes, Gus felt a moment of sadness, an awareness of the years that were slipping out of his own grip, leaving him nothing but scars and weariness to show for them. He told himself that would all change. Today, when he got paid for the mustangs, it would all change.

The redhead was telling the new arrival, "I got him, Eli!"

The graying man, Eli, answered with a curt nod. He scanned Gus, his desperate eyes sharp and appraising. To Edward he said, "What do you think?"

There was hidden meaning in the question. Edward understood it. Scornfully he said, "He claims he found Caesar running loose."

"When I come onto him, he was heading toward the ranch," the redhead volunteered.

Edward grunted, "Shut up, Ned."

Eli considered Gus, then allowed, "Maybe he did find Caesar running loose."

Edward's expression was doubtful.

Gus didn't like these two. He didn't feel like telling them anything. With a mockery of innocence, he said, "I got a notion this here is a real valuable horse. I expect there's a reward for returning him to his rightful owner."

"You do, do you?" Edward snapped.

"Hold on, Edward," Eli said. "If he's telling us the truth about how he found Caesar, he's right. He ought to be rewarded for returning him. A man like this, a drifter, he generally don't have anything but holes in his poke. With some money to spend, he'd want to travel on to someplace like maybe Denver, and have himself a good time. A man who returns a lost horse like Caesar, he deserves some fun as a reward, doesn't he?"

The redhead, Ned, nodded wistfully, envious of a poke full of cash and a good time in Denver.

Edward didn't look very agreeable. He said, "What if he didn't just *find* Caesar the way he claims?"

"Doesn't matter much. Not if we got Caesar back and this feller has what he wants." Eli turned to Gus. "That's what you want, ain't it, cowboy? To ride on with some money in your poke?"

Eli sounded downright eager to have Gus leave. Eager enough to pay him to go. Wondering if Eli and Edward might have been the two men in the gully last night, Gus replied, "Sure. Only I got business to tend to here first. With Mister Harry Boswick. You know him?"

Edward almost winced.

Eli's eyes narrowed. He scowled at Gus. "What kind of business you got with Mister Harry?"

"I reckon that's rightly between him and me."

"Listen, cowboy—" Eli started, his voice a growl of threat. He stopped himself and glanced at Ned. The redhead was watching and listening curiously. Changing tone, his voice calm and controlled, Eli said, "Ned, you take Caesar on up to the ranch and see him fed and bedded."

Obediently Ned sidled his horse toward Gus and reached for the lead rope. Gus held it back. "I ain't giving this stud over to anybody I don't know has the right to him."

Anger was rising red in Edward's face. He didn't like

being defied. And more. He seemed somehow afraid. He snapped, "He's my horse."

"And just who the hell are you?" Gus said.

"I'm the boss around here!"

Gus gave a shake of his head. "Mister Harry Boswick is the boss around here, and you ain't him."

"To hell with him! You listen to me—"

"Hold on, Edward," Eli interrupted. "Don't let some dumb drifter get your goat. It just ain't worth it."

"I don't want him around," Edward said through his teeth. "I don't want him to see—to bother Papa."

"Easy, easy." Eli sounded like he was trying to settle a wild horse. He turned to Gus, going on in the same soothing way. "We don't mean you trouble, cowboy. We're just trying to be helpful. You're from Texas, ain't you?"

"Uh huh." Gus wondered what that had to do with anything.

"Ever been up here to Colorado before?"

"Uh huh."

"This is hard country up here. The winters get colder than hell. You'll freeze your tail off here in the winter."

"It ain't winter now. It ain't gonna be for a while yet."

"Winter comes quicker than you might think. A feller like you wouldn't want to be around these parts in the winter. You want to be back south. Way south. You want to go back right quick. You can go with a reward for finding Caesar, no trouble at all." Eli looked Gus up and down. "Feller like you, likely he draws about forty and found. Right?"

Gus nodded.

Eli asked Edward, "Forty dollars? That ain't too much, is it?"

"No," Edward grumbled reluctantly. "I guess I can spare that much."

Eli grinned at Gus, stretching his mouth wide across his teeth. "How about it, cowboy? A month's wage for a few minutes' work?"

As if he were considering the offer, Gus drawled, "It ain't much for a fine horse like this one."

"Hell, it's as much as you'd make in a month of eating dust punching cattle," Eli protested.

"Yeah," Gus agreed. "Only I ain't punching cattle now. I'm selling horses."

Eli was having trouble keeping the friendly look on his face. "You're not selling that horse, cowboy. You got no claim on him."

"No, not this one. But I got me a herd back up the road a piece that I mean to sell to Mister Boswick. Once I've settled my business with him, I'll be right glad to take that reward and move on."

"Good God!" Edward groaned. "You're *that* damned Texan."

Gus grinned. "Yeah."

"Eli—" Edward started.

Eli shushed him with a gesture, and said to Gus, "You're wasting your time, cowboy. Mister Harry doesn't want to buy any horses. There ain't no need for you to bother yourself with going to the ranch."

"He said he wanted them," Gus answered. "I seen him last year in Dodge and made a deal with him. Now I got his ponies for him, just like he wanted. I reckon he'll see me about them."

"He changed his mind. He doesn't want them," Eli said. "If I were you, I'd take them on somewheres else."

Edward nodded in agreement.

Gus said, "I expect if he don't want them, he can tell me so himself."

"Dammit!" Edward exploded. "We don't want your damned horses. Can't you understand that?"

"I understand *you* don't want them. And I'm getting a notion you just plain don't want me to talk to Mister Boswick. I'm beginning to wonder why."

"Look you—!"

Again Eli interrupted Edward. His voice placating, he said, "Cowboy, we don't want anybody bothering Mister Harry. There's been some—some troubles. He's had enough trouble without you bothering him over some damnfool horses."

"What kind of troubles?" Gus asked.

"That's none of your business!" Edward said.

Eli kept on trying to sound pleasant and reasonable. But his tone hardened as he spoke. "Now, you listen to me, cowboy. Mister Harry doesn't need the worriment of a bunch of new horses on the place, and we want to protect him from it. If you don't want yourself a mess of trouble, you'll head them on down the trail and out of this valley. You understand me?"

Gus grinned slowly. "Hell, I don't mind a little trouble if there's a good profit in it. Mister Harry Boswick offered me a price, and I mean to collect."

He turned to Ned. The young rider was listening and watching in fascination. Whatever secrets Edward and Eli shared, Ned was no party to them. If there were sudden violence now, Ned would be a witness. Or a victim. Gus thought Eli wouldn't want that. Ned's presence would be protection against a bullet in the back. He said, "Ned, maybe you and me might better take Mister Harry this studhorse of his."

Ned looked uncertainly to Eli or Edward for orders. Eli caught breath and sighed. Reluctantly he nodded.

Gus lifted rein to ride on. Ned fell in at his side. Behind them, Eli and Edward exchanged whispers.

3

Gus rode toward the ranch with Ned silent by his side. He could sense that Ned wasn't sure whether he might not be bringing trouble to the ranch.

Gus didn't figure on taking trouble anywhere if he could help it. He didn't care whether or not Edward and Eli had been the men leading the stallion through the night. Not as long as they left him alone. He just wanted to sell his mustangs and get on home. Despite the curiosity that stirred in him, he didn't intend to stay at the ranch any longer than he had to, or mix in anybody else's business any which way.

Still, there was no reason not to try for a few answers as long as it didn't cost him anything. He asked Ned, "That Edward, he's Mister Harry Boswick's son?"

"Uh huh," Ned allowed.

"He don't act much like a rich man."

"He ain't rich, exactly."

"How do you mean?"

"I don't reckon it's my place to talk about him."

Gus agreed, "I reckon not."

But Ned had an urge to talk. And some things about Edward were common ranch gossip. After a few moments he said, "Thing is, Mister Edward is a working hand, same as the rest of us, even if he is Mister Harry's son. He sleeps in the foreman's quarters at the bunkhouse and draws a wage the same as if he was just a hired hand. He don't get no special privileges out of being Mister Harry's boy."

Gus lifted a brow. "You don't say?"

27

Ned nodded. "Mister Harry ain't no ordinary Englishman. He's took to this country real good. He rides kinda funny but he can stay his saddle. The way I hear, he took a mind to raise up his boy to fit the country. He figured making a cowpuncher out of Edward was the way to do it. He's made a top hand out of Edward all right. Edward is the foreman here now, and a damned good man at his job. Only he don't give his pa no lot of thanks for it."

"Kinda resents Mister Harry?" Gus asked.

"I wouldn't say that," Ned drawled. His tone said he would think it though.

"I reckon I wouldn't take it too kindly if my pa was to treat me like a hired hand," Gus commented. He glanced back. Edward and Eli still huddled together talking. There was no sign yet of Dolph and the herd.

"Mister Edward's all right as long as he ain't been at the bottle too hard," Ned was saying. "He ain't an easy boss, but he ain't a hard one, and he can top a randy bronc or drop a loop just as good as if he'd been borned right here in this country."

"That Eli ain't no kin, is he?"

"Eli Tyler?" Ned grinned. "Not yet he ain't."

"How's that?" Gus asked.

Ned started to answer. But he stopped himself as they came within sight of the house. "I reckon it ain't none of my business."

Gus looked at the house ahead. There was a woman standing on the gallery, shading her eyes as she peered toward them. She was short and heavy-set, black-haired, with an Indian look about her. He asked, "Who's that?"

"Housekeeper. Her name's Maria. She's pure Crow."

The woman turned and went into the house.

There was no sign of anyone else. Gus said, "It's right quiet, ain't it?"

"Everybody's out looking for Caesar. Even the Coosie got roped into the hunt. He didn't much take to it. But Mister Harry was upset something fierce when he found out Ceasar'd been stolen." Ned suddenly looked askance at Gus. "I don't see how Caesar could have got out of his stall without he had help."

"Maybe he did have," Gus agreed amiably. "Maybe the thieves got spooked and let him loose."

"Maybe." Ned sounded doubtful. "Mister, I hope to hell you ain't trying to chouse Mister Harry somehow. Nobody around here would take kindly to that. You know what I mean?"

"I reckon I do," Gus said as they rode into the yard.

"Over here." Ned laid rein to his mount's neck, heading for a corral. Reaching it, he dismounted and pulled back the gate poles for Gus to let the stud in.

Gus loosed the horse and began coiling his rope. Ned shoved the poles back into place. The stud trotted around the corral, sniffing and examining it as if he were afraid it had changed while he was gone.

Behind him, Gus heard footsteps. Small, running steps tapping across the hardpacked earth of the yard. Turning, he saw a girl coming toward him.

She clutched her long skirts in both hands and trotted toward the corral with the grace of a fine young filly. A thoroughbred. She was small and slender, with a mass of pale yellow hair caught in ribbons at the back of her head. She looked very young, hardly more than a child.

"Oh, Ned you found him!" she called, her voice filled with delight.

Ned's ears blossomed red. A grin spread itself across his face. He jerked off his hat and stammered, "Yes, ma'am—uh—no, ma'am. It was this feller as found him." He gave a nod at Gus.

The girl stopped short and collected herself. Suddenly demure, she looked at Gus. Her face showed a kinship to Edward, a similarity of line. But in her face the line was far more delicate. The skin was smooth and fashionably pale. The mouth was full and pink. Her eyes were blue, like bits of the bright sky.

Looking into those eyes, Gus sensed some deep sorrow hidden behind the joy of this moment. And he knew she wasn't a child, but a woman.

He pulled off his hat to her. "Ma'am."

Ned nudged him and asked, "What did you say your name was?"

"Gus Widner."

"Miss Vicky," Ned told the girl, "this here is Gus Widner, from Texas. He's a *mesteñero*. He found Caesar and fetched him home."

She smiled graciously and held a small hand out to Gus. "I'm Victoria Boswick. Caesar is my father's favorite horse. I'm grateful to you for bringing him home. We were terribly worried about him, you know."

"Yes, ma'am." Gus touched the outheld hand. He was almost afraid to grasp it. It looked so small and fine that he felt as if his grip might damage it. He knew better, but he still felt that way.

It had been a long ride from Texas. A lonesome sort of ride. During it, he had dreamed a lot about women. Soft and pink and sweet-smelling women like this one. He downright ached as he looked at her. He felt like a damned fool.

"Papa will want to thank you himself for finding Caesar," she was saying, her voice lilting, almost a song. "I'm certain he'll want to reward you."

Gus cleared his throat and asked, "Where is he?"

"He went out with the men hunting Caesar. He must have gone too far to hear that shot. Oh, Ned, when I heard that, I just knew Caesar had been found! I sent Maria out to watch. Ned, will you go see if you can find Papa and tell him?"

"Yes, ma'am." Ned blushed again. Eager to please, he swung onto his horse and galloped away.

Vicky turned to Gus again. "If you don't mind, may I ask, what is a *mesteñero?*"

"A mustanger." He thought of Dolph and the herd as he said it. Glancing uproad, he saw no sign of the horses. Or of Edward and Eli. He felt vaguely uneasy about that.

"Mustanger?" Vicky repeated the word as if she

weren't familiar with it. "You have something to do with the native wild horses?"

"I catch them. Sell them. I got a bunch coming in now. They should be here right soon."

"Are those the *Texas cayuses* that Papa ordered last year?" She sounded as if she were experimenting with a foreign language she was just learning.

"Yes, ma'am. I reckon so. I seen him in Dodge about them last year."

Her face sparkled with girlish delight. "Wonderful! Papa was wondering if they'd come. I'm dying to see them. Are they much different from our horses here?"

"Well, they got four legs and a tail apiece. At least they did last time I seen them. But you wouldn't mistake none of them for that Caesar horse you got there."

She smiled and nodded with satisfaction. "That's what Papa wants. Something really different. He wants to get as many different types of horses as he can."

"Why?" Gus asked. He was enjoying talking with her.

"He's experimenting with horsebreeding. Are you familiar with the work of Gregor Johann Mendel?"

He shook his head. He couldn't recollect he had ever heard the name before.

"Oh." She seemed disappointed. Then she smiled, as if it didn't really matter. "Well, it has to do with breeding plants. Papa is interested in how it might apply to horses. He wants to get a lot of different kinds of horses for his experiments. He has some fascinating ideas connected with Mister Darwin's theories. He thinks he might be able to breed back to the primal horse, as well as breed ahead to a superior horse of the future. It's all very exciting."

Gus wasn't sure what she was talking about, but he grinned with amusement at her enthusiasm. She was a pretty little thing. But even in her excitement, the dark sorrow lingered deep in her eyes. He wondered what could have caused it.

"Oh, look!" She suddenly pointed toward the road. "Are those your Texas cayuses?"

Turning, Gus saw the herd coming into sight. Dolph wasn't driving the mustangs alone. He had the help of half a dozen riders. Two of them were Edward and Eli. He supposed the others were ranch hands who had been out hunting the stud and had found Dolph instead. They were moving the mustangs along at a lope.

"Yes, ma'am," he answered Vicky. "Where do you want them?"

She glanced around. "In that big corral, I suppose. Will it hold them all?"

"For the time being. But they ain't much for being penned up long. They get to sulling." Gus headed for the corral she had indicated. He pulled down the bars so that the herd could be driven in.

Vicky followed him. She stood close beside him, watching in fascination as the mustangs loped toward her. Sounding happy about it, she said, "They *are* different! So many colors!"

"Yes, ma'am, they—"

Something happened.

It happened suddenly, and Gus didn't see what it was. He just saw that suddenly the herd exploded. Suddenly the mustangs were running hard, stampeding toward him.

Vicky jerked up a hand to cover her mouth. Her wide eyes stared as the horses thundered toward her. She seemed frozen in a moment of awed surprise.

The mustangs lunged, frantic in their fright. They were close. In an instant they would be on top of her.

Gus flung himself against her, throwing her down, grabbing her, rolling with her clutched in his arms.

The bottom corral rail was set high enough for a man to duck under it. Gus rolled Vicky under it. But there was no safety inside the corral. Some of the panicked mustangs had gone on in and were racing circles along the fence.

Gus held the girl there on the ground, under the rail, as hooves rattled past. He felt clods of hoof-flung earth hit against his back. Against his chest he felt the warmth of the girl's body. His arms around her felt the throbbing of her heart, the heaving of her lungs. Her stays were light, her blouse and camisole soft and thin. He was aware of the small breasts under them, firm and intriguing.

Then the mustangs were past, and she was struggling against his arms. He let go and rolled back. Rising, he offered her his hand.

She scrambled up without his help.

The ribbons had come loose and her hair was a wild tangle of pale gold. Giving her head a toss, she brushed it back from her face. There was dirt on her face, and on her clothing. The top button of her blouse had come open, showing a small triangle of pale flesh at the base of her throat. It looked very smooth, very kissable. Gus tried not to stare at it.

Behind the smudges, her face was burning red.

"I'm sorry, ma'am," he said. "Only they might have run you down."

She tried to say something. She seemed too embarrassed to find words. Wheeling away from Gus, she gathered her soiled skirts and hurried toward the house. Her stride was long and stiff and angry.

On the gallery, she paused. She looked back. And then she was gone into the house.

Gus wondered what had made her so angry. Had she sensed his thoughts as he held her close? Or was she mad at herself because she'd had thoughts of her own there in his arms? She was a hell of a pretty little thing. It would be right nice to have her fancy him.

His palms were very sweaty. He wiped them down his pants' legs.

The riders had the runaway mustangs bunched and were driving them into the corral. Gus gave a hand with the gate poles. As he slid the last pole into place, he heard one of the riders call out, "Here comes Mister Harry now!"

Turning, he saw Ned and a couple of other riders loping up the road toward the yard. They all wore range clothes, but even at a distance it was easy enough to spot Harry Boswick. He was a small man, but he rode tall, in a straight-backed, high-headed way. The horse under him was a big one, with a look of thoroughbred blood, but a rangier, heavier animal than the stud, Caesar. Too heavy an animal for a good cowpony, Gus thought.

As the riders approached, Gus could see the differences in their clothing. Boswick's duck breeches and cotton shirt were off a store shelf, as worn and faded as the ones the others wore, but his vest was Indian tanned buckskin with a lot of fancy beadwork on it. Instead of a Bull tag, a watch fob hung from one pocket. His Stetson didn't look like he had ever watered his horse out of it. There were no scars of thorns or rope burns across his knuckles. Small things, but they spoke of money, the difference between a rich boss and a common hired hand.

Harry Boswick rode a short rein with a shankless bit. He held his reins in both hands. As he came up in front of Gus, he halted the horse with slight twists of his wrists.

Stopping at Boswick's side, Ned aimed a finger at Gus. "This here is the feller who found Caesar!"

Boswick beamed at Gus. His look was excited and childlike, much the same as Vicky's had been. "You're the Texan I met in Dodge City!"

"Yes sir," Gus said.

Suddenly Eli was trotting up to Boswick's side. His voice taut, he said, "Mister Harry, I got to talk to you!"

"In a minute."

"But this is—"

"Later, Eli." Boswick turned away from Eli, the motion dismissing him. Pulling off his Stetson, he wiped at his face with a bandana. His face was as tanned and weathered as an old cowhand's. His thinning yellow hair was fading white, streaked and stained by the sun. His eyes were the same sky blue as Vicky's. Gus looked into them, hunting a reflection of the sorrow he had seen in

Vicky's eyes. He didn't find it. Whatever her burden, she didn't share it with her father.

"You've brought my *Texas cayuses!*" Boswick said enthusiastically, using the words in the same way Vicky had, as if they were a new language, and the mustangs new toys. He had lost a lot of his accent, but not enough to pass himself off as anything but an Englishman. He seemed to be trying to lose it all. "I'm happy to see you, Mister—uh—Weiser, is it?"

"Widner. Gus Widner."

"A pleasure to see you again, Mister Widner."

Dolph had ridden up. Dismounting, he stepped to Gus's side. Gus hooked a thumb at him. "This here is my brother, Dolph."

"My pleasure." Boswick beamed at Dolph for a moment, then looked toward the mustangs in the corral. Edging his mount closer, he eyed them critically over the rails.

The mustangs were all small, for the most part just pony-sized. They were heavy-headed and short-legged with stubby necks, mostly ewed. They were a colorful lot, patches and pintos, buckskins and duns, roans and sorrels, with a few bays and a fleabitten gray. Some had feathered legs and the duns showed some zebra striping. All had long, thick manes and brushy tails, matted and tangled. Compared to the horses on Boswick's ranch, they were a scraggly, runty, moth-eaten looking lot.

"They're—ah—interesting," Boswick observed. "A little like moor ponies."

Gus didn't know anything about moor ponies. But he caught a hint of disappointment in Boswick's voice. He said, "They're what you asked for. They're real wild ones. Except for our using ponies that are mixed in with them, there ain't a one in that bunch has ever had a saddle on its back or a bit in its mouth. They might not look like much to you, Mister Boswick, but they'll fight you like hell, and when you've got them licked, they'll work like hell for you. They'll fatten on forage and eat prickly pears with the spikes on. They'll keep happy in land where that horse you're sitting would dry up and die in just a few days."

"Will they really?" Boswick sounded hopeful, but not at all certain Gus wasn't spinning him a windy.

"Try them," Gus answered.

Dolph had been eying the mustangs critically himself, aware that they made a poor show next to Boswick's horses. For a moment he had felt ashamed of them. Now he grinned and nodded proudly in agreement with his brother.

"Yes, I will," Boswick said.

"There's forty-eight mares and fillies there," Gus told him. "Ten or fifteen of the mares are old enough to be carrying for the stud we stole them from. The rest are old enough to kick and bite and forage for themselves. The geldings in with them are our using ponies. We lost one on the way here, so I'm keeping back a mare to pack home with. That leaves you forty-seven head. That suit you, Mister Boswick?"

"Yes."

"Our agreement was for fifty dollars a head delivered. I allow that comes to—" Gus paused. He had calculated it all time and time again on the ride up. Now he had to deduct for the mare he was keeping.

"Fifty dollars a head!" Eli exploded. His face darkened with anger. "For those crowbaits? That's outright thievery!"

Gus glared at him. "Fifty dollars a head is what me and Mister Boswick agreed on back to Dodge. That's why I brought these ponies all the way here from Texas."

"Those nags wouldn't be worth ten dollars a head if they were all broke to rope and cut and to do the two-step," Eli snapped.

"Maybe back home they wouldn't be worth ten dollars a head," Gus admitted frankly. "But we've went to a hell of a lot of work to get just exactly what Mister Boswick wanted, and we've fetched them a hell of a long way over some rough country."

He looked at Boswick. "You and me bargained a price last year, and me and Dolph worked our butts to the bone to get you just what you said you wanted, and trail-broke them and got them across the plains and the mountains, and now here they are. Do you and me have a deal or don't we?"

"Hell, I could have got all the damned Texas mustangs you want off trailherd remudas up to Wyoming for ten dollars a head," Eli told his boss. He seemed as indignant as if it were his money Boswick meant to throw away on the mustangs. "They'd have been all broke and ready for using."

"I don't want using stock," Boswick answered. "I want authentic wild stock, born and bred in the wilderness. Not ranch-reared animals subject to intrusions of mixed blood."

"All mustangs got mixed blood," Eli grumbled. "Ranch horses all the time run off and mix with them. The best ones got some ranch blood in them."

"Not for my purposes," Boswick said. He turned to Gus again. "Do you warrant these animals are from the wilderness where any intrusion of non-cayuse blood is unlikely?"

"Mister, there ain't a man alive can guarantee you any wild mustang ain't had a ranch horse somewhere in the family. Some folks say they're all come from Spanish stock. But me and Dolph went halfway to hell to find you ponies from where there wasn't another white man within a hundred miles of their range. I expect none of that bunch ever laid eyes on a man, white or red, before we took them. That's what you said you wanted, and that's what we got you. You got my word on that."

"If they never saw a man before, it's because they ain't worth a man bothering with them," Eli muttered.

"I want them," Boswick said. "I made a bargain for them at a price and I believe they're worth every cent of it. Forty-seven cayuses at fifty dollars a head is twenty-three hundred and fifty dollars. Correct, Mister Widner?"

"Yes sir," Gus said, his voice mostly breath. That was a hell of a lot of money. As often as he had tallied it, the amount still awed him. It was more than he and Dolph could earn between them in three, four years of chousing longhorns out of the brush or topping broncs for some rancher back home in Texas. A hell of a lot of money.

Boswick seemed unconcerned over the amount, as if there were plenty more where that came from. He swung down from his tall horse and handed the reins to Ned. Like a longtime rannihan, he was bowlegged. The top of his head came about even with Gus's nose. But he stood tall, with dignity—the natural dignity that came from the power of money and an inbred belief in his own quality.

Glancing around, he asked, "Where is Edward?"

"He was here a while ago," Eli said.

"I want him to see these cayuses."

"He won't like them."

Boswick didn't answer that, but turned to Gus and Dolph. "Come along to the house and we'll drink to these Texas cayuses of yours."

4

The front door was standing open. As Boswick led the brothers up onto the gallery, Gus could hear a voice within the house. It was Vicky's, and she sounded upset. Her tone was pleading.

"No, Edward! Please don't. You know you shouldn't drink so much!"

"Dammit, don't go telling me what I shouldn't do!" Edward answered. "I do what I damned well please!"

"Edward?" Boswick called as he reached the doorway. He was giving warning, giving Edward and Vicky a chance to compose themselves.

He led Gus and Dolph into a large parlor. Vicky and Edward were across the room. Edward had a bottle in his hand. Vicky had been facing her brother, but at Boswick's call she had turned. She took a step forward, coming between Edward and Boswick, as if she meant to hide Edward from her father's sight.

Edward had no intention of hiding. Defiantly he put the bottle to his mouth and swallowed. The Adam's apple worked jerkily in his throat. He looked as if he'd had more than one swallow from that bottle already.

Quietly Boswick said, "Edward, those Texas cayuses I ordered are here. They're out in the big corral. I want you to go take a look at them."

Edward lowered the bottle. He stood hesitantly, as if he considered refusing. Slowly he wiped his mouth with the back of his hand. Then he set down the bottle. With just a trace of a nod, he strode past his sister. Past Boswick. Gus stepped back, making way for him. Dolph was standing in the doorway. He didn't move quickly enough. Edward reached him before he had stepped clear. Giving him a hard shove, Edward strode on past him.

"Hey!" Dolph grunted. Anger flashed in his eyes. He tensed as if he meant to go after Edward and shove back.

"Hold on, brother," Gus growled softly. His tone was an order that demanded to be obeyed.

Reluctantly Dolph eased back. He and Vicky looked at each other. She seemed startled by him, perhaps by his resemblance to his brother. He was obviously pleased by her. Grinning at her, he pulled off his hat.

"Vicky," Boswick said, his voice still calm and level as if nothing at all were unusual, "I want to introduce the Widner brothers. This is Dolph, and this is Gus."

She smiled at Dolph, making a small curtsey, then looked at Gus. Color rose to her cheeks. Her eyes touched his for an instant, then darted away. Catching up her skirts, she said, "Please excuse me."

Whirling, she dashed away.

Boswick lifted a brow at Gus. There were questions in his eyes. But he didn't speak them. He said, "Come on into my office."

The parlor he led them through was a wide, broad room with a beamed ceiling. A staircase climbed one wall. A huge stone fireplace stood against the opposite wall. The mantel held an assortment of stuffed birds, raw rock, and Indian gear. Over it hung the head of a bull buffalo, glowering glassily. More heads of smaller game peered from the other walls, with stretched pelts, firearms, tomahawks, and war shields crowded among them. Bear hides with heads attached showed false teeth in frozen snarls around the floor.

Boswick's office opened off the parlor. It was a much smaller room than the parlor, but by Gus's standards it was big. Like the parlor, it had a stone fireplace and a mantel crammed with oddities. Glass-fronted cabinets held books and curios. The front end of a bobcat mounted in mid-leap, teeth bared and claws out-stretched, hung over a small iron safe. The cat was cut off just behind the ribs, and looked as if it were plunging through the wall.

Across from the safe was a roll-top desk, and next to that an oak table holding a large machine, the like of which Gus had never seen before. It was a high-backed wooden box with a framework of some kind rising from it. There was a wheel sort of thing inside, and rods and springs, and in front four rows of studs or buttons with letters of the alphabet on them.

Nudging Gus, Dolph nodded at the thing and whispered, "What the hell is that contraption?"

Gus shrugged.

Boswick had overheard. Smiling pleasantly, sounding proud, he said, "That is a Pratt Patented Pterotype machine."

"A what?" Gus asked.

"A Pterotype machine," Boswick repeated. "It is a device for making instantly printed copy without the use of hand-set type or a press. Here, I'll show you."

Opening the roll-top desk, he took out a sheet of black carboned paper and a blank sheet of white paper. Putting the two sheets face to face, he attached them to the framework of the machine. He did something at the side of the device that caused a noise inside it, then pressed down one of the studs. Things inside the machine jumped. The frame gave a little jerk. Boswick pressed another stud. The machine did it all again. He kept pressing studs and the machine kept jumping and jerking. Then he pulled out the papers and peeled the carboned sheet off the white sheet.

The white sheet wasn't blank anymore. Now a row of words staggered across it, looking a lot like something in a newspaper.

Gus gazed at it in fascination. His lips moved slightly as he spelled out the letters. The words were his own name, and Dolph's.

"How did it do that?" he asked, impressed.

"It's a very complicated mechanism. Very simple to operate but impossible to explain," Boswick said, smiling apologetically. "It was made in London, but it was invented by a countryman of yours. An Alabaman named John Pratt."

Gus didn't know Pratt. He had never been to Alabama. He thought if he ever got over that way, he'd like to look up Pratt and ask him about the workings of the machine.

"Mister Boswick," Dolph was saying, "you reckon maybe me and Gus could borrow the loan of that piece of paper a while? I sure would like to take it home and show it to Ma and Pa."

"It's yours." Boswick handed it to him.

"We'll pay you for it," Gus said as Dolph accepted the paper.

"No, please, take it as a gift from me," Boswick said.

"Obliged," Dolph grinned. Folding the paper carefully, he stuck it inside his hat.

Boswick gestured at the horsehide armchairs grouped by the desk. "Please make yourselves comfortable. Drinks?"

"Obliged," Gus said. He settled himself into one of the chairs. It was deep and soft. He wondered why nobody had ever built a saddle soft like that.

Still standing, Dolph looked around. "Sir, if you don't mind me asking, did you kill all these critters around here yourself?"

Boswick was opening one of the cabinets, taking out a cut-glass decanter and drinking glasses. He glanced up and saw that Dolph was looking at the mounted trophies on the walls.

"No," he admitted. "Some are my own. Some were purchased. I'm rather a bit of an amateur naturalist, you know. At least I dabble in it. I purchased a number of specimens of indigenous American wildlife for my studies. They give the place rather a *native* air, don't you think?"

Dolph nodded blankly. He wasn't sure he had caught Boswick's drift at all.

"My wife didn't care much for them," Boswick said, sounding sad about it.

Gus felt inclined to agree with the wife. The room was downright spooky with all those dead animals staring at you from every corner. It gave him the same kind of feeling as an Indian holy place, all full of fetishes and the spirits of the dead.

Boswick held a drink out to him. Accepting, he took a sample sip. It was some kind of corn whisky, but very soft and mellow. No bite to it at all. He downed it, feeling a little like he was swallowing sarsaparilla. No bite and no kick. He thought a pinch of chili and a couple of rattler heads might have perked it up.

Boswick gave a drink to Dolph and took one for himself. He sipped, then beamed at Gus as if he were downright proud of the stuff.

"Now about the money," Boswick said, reaching to open a desk drawer. "I'll make out a draft on my bank for you."

Dolph looked to Gus. "We ain't gonna get paid in *paper*, are we?"

Gus didn't want to offend Boswick. But he sure as hell didn't want paper either. He licked his lips and said to Boswick, "We'd be obliged for hard money."

"Hard money?" Boswick repeated the words as if he didn't understand them.

"Gold!" Doph said sharply.

Boswick did take offense then. "I assure you, my bank draft is as good as gold in any nation on earth."

"Not in Texas, it ain't!" Dolph protested. "We worked for *money,* and we want *money,* not a wad of kindling!"

Boswick started to reply. Gus waved a hand at him, gesturing for silence. Something had made a small noise just outside the open office door. Rising, with his hand on the butt of his revolver, Gus started for the door. His spurs jangled at each step.

"Boss?" Eli Tyler's voice called. Eli stepped into the doorway, coming face to face with Gus. He glared at Gus a moment, then looked past him to ask, "Boss, is something wrong? I thought I heard shouting."

"No," Boswick said. "Nothing's wrong."

Gus was certain Eli had been shouldered up against the wall next to the door eavesdropping. Glaring at Eli, he said, "It ain't none of your concern."

Eli answered his gaze with silent challenge.

Boswick, too, suspected Eli of spying. He didn't like it. His tone was cold, a harsh dismissal. "Eli, would you see to it that Caesar is being properly tended?"

Eli sucked breath between his teeth. It was an order from the boss. Obeying reluctantly, he turned and stalked off.

Gus waited in the doorway, watching until Eli was gone from the parlor. Then he closed the door and turned to Boswick again.

Boswick was standing by the desk, refreshing his drink. He took a taste of it, then said, "Just what is your objection to my bank draft?"

"Back home we got Confederate money and shin plasters enough to burn for our cook fires," Gus told him. "Folks down home don't use paper money anymore. Nobody will take it. Nobody trusts it. We had it go bad on us during the war, and then again in the Panic of Seventy-Three. Now nobody back home wants no more of it."

"That's foolish. The currency is sound. My bank is sound. My draft is as good as gold."

"That might be so today, but by the time we get home again, there ain't no telling. Banks can go busted. They've done it on us before and I reckon they'll do it on us again. It could be we'll have another panic. Mister Boswick, me and Dolph have folks back home and we have debts the carpetbaggers put on the family ten years ago that we ain't been able to get out from under yet. We've been counting on this money you promised for the mustangs. If your bank draft is as good as gold, it shouldn't hurt you to give us gold instead."

"Would it?" Dolph asked.

"No," Boswick admitted. "I suppose not. I—I'm rather afraid I misunderstood your position, Mister Widner. I mistook your attitude as mistrust of me. Please accept my apologies."

"You'll give us gold?"

"Certainly, if it's so important to you. However, I must warn you, it's hardly safe to carry such sums in gold in this part of the country. Why, just a few days ago someone broke into my house and attempted to rob my safe." He indicated the little iron box under the stuffed bobcat.

"We'll take our chances," Gus told him.

"All right. I wish you well. But I don't keep anything like that much cash in hand. Not since the robbery attempt. We can go into town in the morning and I'll get the money for you from the bank. You will be my guests here on the ranch tonight, won't you?"

Dolph scowled in disappointment. "I meant to go into town tonight."

"What for?" Gus said. "You ain't got two bits to spend on beer and wimmen."

Boswick made a small noise of understanding. "If you would like, I can give you an advance on—no—I certainly owe you some reward for bringing Caesar back to me. I'll gladly pay you that in—ah—*hard money* right now. Would you consider a hundred dollars a fair reward?"

"A hundred dollars!" The words whistled from Dolph's mouth, and his eyes widened. He looked like he was already seeing all that beer, all those women.

Gus grinned at his brother. He was thinking of a stallion to start a herd for the family. He and Dolph could split the hundred dollars reward and have themselves enough fun to pay them for the long ride. Then maybe it wouldn't hurt so much if they pooled their share of the mustang money to buy a stud.

"Yes, sir!" he said to Boswick. "That would be just fine."

Stepping to the safe, Boswick knelt and pulled open the door. It hadn't been locked. He took out a small box and slid back the lid. The box was full of silver, with a few gold coins mixed in. It looked like several hundred dollars to Gus. That seemed like a lot of money to keep in an unlocked safe. But he supposed a man like Boswick thought more in thousands than hundreds.

Curious, he asked, "What kind of a stud fee do you get for that Caesar horse?"

"Stud fee? I really wouldn't know. I've never put Caesar up to stud for a fee," Boswick said. "I've only bred him for my own purposes."

"You sell his colts?"

"Occasionally, yes."

"What kind of price?"

"I let the last one go for eight hundred. A yearling. I sold it to a friend."

Gus sighed. Eight hundred was more than he and Dolph could pool, even if they included every cent of the reward money. And they couldn't take it out of the rest of the mustang money. They had to go for debts, and for family necessities.

"Were you interested in buying a colt?" Boswick asked.

"Can't help but be interested," Gus admitted. "Only I reckon Caesar's blood is a little rich for us."

Boswick had picked a handful of coins from the box. He returned the box to the safe and swung the door shut. As he started to rise, he said, "Perhaps we could—"

The sound of a shot slammed through the office window.

Boswick flinched. He staggered forward, a frown wrinkling his forehead. His face drained pale and his eyes glazed. With a strangling sound, he fell toward Gus.

Catching him, lowering him to the floor, Gus snapped, "Dolph, he's shot! Look to him!"

Dolph dropped to his knees at Boswick's side. Gus stepped over the downed man and strode to the window. He pressed himself against the wall beside it. Automatically he had drawn his revolver. He held it at ready as he took a quick look out the window.

There was no one in sight.

The shot had come from some distance. A rifle shot. The most likely place seemed to be a wooded knoll across the yard, upslope a ways, a part of the woodlot. Staring at the knoll, he thought he saw something move among the trees.

It was too far a throw for the old Leech & Rigdon. And Gus felt the hammer slack under his thumb. As he remembered the broken spring, he mumbled a curse. But there were rifles and shotguns racked in the parlor. If the man on the knoll were afoot, maybe he could grab one and get out there in time to snap off a shot.

Even as the thoughts flashed through his mind, he heard the clatter of hard heels coming through the parlor toward the office.

"Boss?" Eli Tyler shouted. The office door slammed open and Eli was standing there, his pistol in his hand.

He started, sucking a hard breath as he saw Boswick on the floor. There was blood on Boswick's vest. Coins lay around his outstretched hand. Shining silver and gold. Dolph was on his knees at Boswick's side, looking as if he meant to help the injured man. Or maybe to gather up the spilled coins.

Gus was at the window. He had wheeled as Eli broke into the room. His revolver was in one hand. There was blood on the other.

Eli's gun was already leveled at Gus's gut. Through his teeth he ordered, "Drop it, mister!"

5

So Eli Tyler hadn't fired that shot, Gus thought. But Eli had arrived in a hell of a hurry. The shot had been fired from the knoll outside. That was the place that should have drawn attention. And here was Eli busting into the office with his gun already in his hand, set for trouble. Either Eli had been expecting the shot, or he had been in the parlor spying on the office. Maybe both.

Gus gestured toward the knoll beyond the window. "He's out there. He's getting away."

"Drop that gun," Eli repeated, his voice demanding. He meant to shoot if he wasn't obeyed. And he could probably get away with it, shooting a man he'd found gun in hand standing over his wounded boss.

But Gus was damned sure Eli knew he hadn't shot Boswick. He wondered if Eli wanted the man who had done it to escape. In the time Eli had already wasted, the man could be well away from the knoll, losing himself in the woods, or mingling with the ranch hands.

And now it was too late to go chasing after him.

With a disgusted sigh, Gus slipped the broken revolver back into his holster and dropped to one knee at the downed man's side. He asked Dolph, "How bad is it?"

Dolph had a hand on Boswick's brow. He gave an uncertain shake of his head. "I can't tell. He's cold like he was dead, but he don't exactly feel dead."

Gus pushed his brother's hand aside to feel the face for himself. The skin was cold and damp and waxy pale. But there was life in it. Glancing toward Eli, he said, "Fetch some blankets quick."

"Keep your hands off him!" Eli waved his gun in threat.

Gus snapped, "Fetch some blankets, dammit!"

Eli looked uncertain. He asked, "He's not dead?"

"No. But he will be if he ain't tended. Fetch some blankets, dammit!"

Suddenly someone was pushing past Eli, rushing into the office. It was the Crow woman Gus has seen on the gallery when he first arrived.

At the sight of her, Eli shouted at Gus, "Damn you, you've killed Mister Harry!"

Gus spoke to the Crow woman. "He's not dead. Fetch some blankets."

She looked at Boswick, met Gus's eyes, and nodded. Turning, she hurried away.

Gus looked at Eli then. Under the heavy tan, Eli's face was pale. He was blinking rapidly. Trying hard to think quick and straight, Gus decided. Confused because things weren't going the way he had expected.

Gus said, "The bullet that hit Mister Boswick was meant for me, wasn't it?"

Eli blinked. And scowled. "How the hell should I know?"

"What do you mean?" Dolph asked his brother.

"I was on my feet here on this side of Boswick, away from the window," Gus said. "Boswick was hunkered down at the safe. Whoever was out there had a clear shot at me. Only just as he pulled the trigger, Boswick stood up. He moved into the bullet. If it had been fired a second sooner or he had stood up a second later, it would have hit me. I'm the one it was meant for."

"Hell, Gus—that—that—" Dolph stammered. "For you?"

Gus nodded. He had been watching Eli, trying to read the man's thoughts, looking for some hint of whether Eli had been expecting Gus to be shot at. But there was too much nervousness, too much anger, too much excitement in Eli's face. Gus couldn't read his reaction.

Somewhere in the house a door slammed. Running

footsteps sounded from a distant room. They pattered toward the parlor. Small steps. A woman's steps.

"Eli!" Vicky gasped as she rushed into the office. "What happened? Maria says—"

She didn't finish. At the sight of Boswick on the floor, the breath went out of her. So did the color. Her voice came small and thin, "Papa!"

She looked as if she were fainting. Gus turned to catch her. But she steadied herself. Dropping to her knees, she bent over her father. She touched his face with fingers almost as pale as the cold flesh they felt.

"He's not dead!" She wasn't speaking of certainty. She was protesting the possibility.

"He's not," Gus assured her. "You got a doctor around these parts?"

"Yes." Her hand pressed to her father's face. Her voice was vague, distracted. "He's cold. He's so terribly cold!"

"The Crow woman's gone for blankets. That'll help," Gus told her. He wanted to comfort her. He felt an urge to take her into his arms, or at least take her hand in his. Soothingly he said, "Now we've got to send for a doctor."

"Yes," she agreed. She was struggling to collect herself. "Eli, go and get Doctor Parsons."

Eli obviously didn't want to leave. Waving his gun at Gus and Dolph, he said, "But, ma'am, these men—"

"Hurry! Please!" she interrupted.

"You'd better send for the law, too," Gus suggested. "You got law in these parts?"

"We can stomp our own snakes," Eli snapped at him.

Gus asked his question of Vicky. "You got law in these parts?"

"There's a deputy on the other side of the gap. It's better than a day's ride there and back."

"You'd better send somebody to fetch him."

Vicky spoke to Eli. "Send someone for the deputy. Send someone for the doctor. Please hurry."

"I'll send somebody," he answered her. He glared at

Gus for a moment before he left. His eyes were full of threat. As he stalked away, he called, "I'll be right back!"

Vicky's attention had returned to her father. She said, "He's so pale. So cold. Are you certain he'll be all right?"

Gus wasn't certain. He shouted into the house, "Where's them blankets?"

"Here!" the Crow woman called. She was hurrying through the parlor. She rushed into the office with her arms full of blankets. Dropping them on the floor, she opened one to spread it over Boswick. Vicky started to help her, but the girl's fingers trembled. The blanket slipped out of her grip.

Gus motioned her away and gave the Crow woman a hand. As they tucked the last blanket around Boswick, Gus asked the woman, "Can you make medicine? Make something that will warm his insides?"

She touched Boswick's face, testing the chill of his flesh and considering. With a nod, she rose and left.

Vicky had been watching helplessly. She looked up with a sudden thought. "Shouldn't we get Papa into bed?"

"No," Gus told her. "I don't think we ought to move him until the doctor gets here. Let the doc say what to do."

"Are you sure?" she asked.

As Gus nodded, he heard sounds in the parlor. Eli was back, and there were several ranch hands following him. The men grouped quietly outside the office door, their hats in their hands, their mouths grim and their faces solemn.

Eli pushed on into the office. He had overheard Vicky's question. He demanded, "Sure about what?"

"I thought we should get Papa to bed," she told him.

He turned to the men. "Come on. A couple of you give me a hand getting Mister Harry up to his room."

"No!" Gus snapped as the men started into the office. He had been hunkering at Boswick's side. Rising, he stepped between them and the downed man. They stopped, looking to Eli for a reply.

"What the hell you got to say about it?" Eli grunted at Gus. "You *want* him dead!"

The men muttered among themselves.

Gus answered, "I saw plenty of men shot up in the war, and I've seen a few since. I know if a bullet is in a bad place inside a man, you can make it a hell of a lot worse by jogging him around. You let Mister Boswick lie still now. Let the doctor say what to do about him."

"I think he's right," one of the men volunteered.

Others muttered in agreement.

Eli didn't like it. He spoke to the men. "Are you gonna listen to him? He's the one who shot Mister Harry!"

Vicky looked up at Gus, then at Dolph, then at Gus again, and finally at Eli. "Why would Mister Widner shoot Papa?"

"There ain't no reason," Gus told her. "I didn't do it."

Eli answered her, "For money, that's why! The Boss opened the safe in front of him and he took a notion to help himself out of it!"

The listening ranch hands muttered among themselves.

Gus didn't like the dark sound of their voices. He shook his head in denial. "Mister Boswick told us he didn't keep much money in that safe. He said he didn't have enough cash on hand to pay me and my brother for the mustangs we brought him. He only opened the safe to give us a reward for fetching home that Caesar horse. He was going to have to go in to the bank tomorrow to get us our money. Why would I shoot him to rob a safe of less than he owed us?"

"Likely he changed his mind about paying you so damned much for that wolfbait you wanted to chouse off on him," Eli snapped.

"Eli," Vicky said sternly, as if he had insulted her, "you know that if Papa made a deal he wouldn't go back on it."

Gus could sense that the ranch hands agreed with her.

Eli had to agree too, even if he didn't like it. With a jerk of his head toward Gus, he grumbled, "Well, when I got here he had his gun in his hand and he was over by the window just about to jump out of it and run away."

"This gun?" Gus said, drawing the Leech & Rigdon. Eli flinched as Gus leveled the revolver at him. From the corner of his eye Gus scanned the men crowded at the doorway. One of them was the young rider, Ned. With a flick of his wrist he tossed the gun. "Here, Ned, catch!"

Automatically Ned snatched at the gun. Catching it, he stared at it in puzzlement.

"Try it," Gus told him.

He put his thumb to the hammer. It flopped loose at his touch. Holding it up, he told the men around him, "It's busted."

"You reckon I could have shot Mister Boswick with a busted gun?" Gus said.

Ned shook his head.

"Hell, maybe it busted *after* you shot him," Eli said.

Gus suggested to Ned, "Smell it."

Ned sniffed the gun. "It don't smell like it's been fired lately."

Eli was running out of arguments. He gave a grunt, then glowered at the men. "What the hell you all standing around here for? Ain't none of you got work to do?"

Vicky looked at the men. "I'd like to be alone with Papa."

"Yeah," one of the men said. "Come on, we got work to do."

The men began to drift away. All but Eli. He stood hesitant, not wanting to leave. Or else not wanting to go until Gus and Dolph were gone.

"Come on, Eli, you heard the lady," Gus said to him. With a nod to Vicky, Gus started out of the office.

Dolph paused. His eyes met Vicky's. He gave her a small smile of sympathy.

She answered him with a slight forced smile of her own. An assurance that she was all right.

He joined Gus then, and they walked on through the parlor, with Eli following a few paces behind them. Outside, Gus led Dolph toward the corrals. He scanned the yard and spotted an outhouse off at a distance from the big house.

Leaning close, he whispered to Dolph, "I'm going to take a look at the place that shot was fired from. You keep an eye on Eli. Don't let him trail after me."

"You think he had something to do with the shooting?"

"Maybe. If he did, I don't want him getting up there and messing up any sign before I can see it."

Dolph nodded.

Gus turned away and headed for the outhouse. He went on inside. When he came out again, he could see Dolph perched on a corral rail, looking toward the big house. Eli was nowhere in sight. Angling off from the outhouse, Gus headed for the knoll.

Dolph was still sitting on the corral rail when Gus got back.

"You have any trouble with Eli? Gus asked.

Dolph gave a shake of his head. "You'd just gone in when that Edward came up. Him and Eli went back into the house together. They're still in there. You find anything?"

"Horse droppings. A grain-fed horse. I'd guess it was one of the ranch stock."

"That all?"

"Yeah," Gus said, hoisting himself up to sit beside Dolph. "How did Edward come up? Riding or afoot?"

"Riding."

"Where's his mount?"

"He looped up the reins and slapped it. It went to the barn." Dolph hooked a thumb toward the stable.

"What was it like?"

"Like? Like a horse. Leg on each corner. Tail on one end, head on the other."

"I mean was it a fancy-bred horse like that Caesar?"

"Uh huh. A bay gelding."

"You notice whether there was a saddle gun?"

Dolph pursed his lips as he considered. He shook his head slowly. "I can't say. Didn't pay no mind." He looked up sharply. "You think Edward fired that shot?"

"I think he could have."

"Shoot his own pa? That's—brother, did you say back there you had a notion he'd meant to shoot you?"

"Yeah."

"Why would he want to shoot you?"

"I saw the men stealing that Caesar horse, remember? I didn't get a good enough look to see who they might be, but they can't be sure of that. If it was Edward and Eli, they can pretty well figure it was me who seen them. Maybe they figured it would be worth killing me to keep me from telling Boswick."

"Hell!" Dolph grunted. He scowled as he considered. "Brother, what are we gonna do about it?"

"When that lawman gets here, I'll tell him what I know, and what I think."

"We got to hang around here until he gets here?"

"I reckon we got to hang around until we can collect for these ponies." Gus indicated the mustangs milling in the corral.

"There ain't any chance they'll change their minds about buying the ponies, is there?" Dolph asked.

"I hope not. Eli's right that there isn't anybody but Boswick who would pay more than ten dollars a head for crowbaits like them. If we have to take them back and sell them somewhere else we'll have had us a long ride for damned small pay." Gus looked toward the house. "If Boswick gets well, he'll pay us all right. You heard what Miss Vicky said about her pa keeping his word?"

"Uh huh."

"I expect she's the same cut. It's Edward I'm not sure

of. We'd better hope to hell Boswick doesn't die and leave everything to that son of his."

"I hope he don't die anyway," Dolph said. "I kind of like him."

Eying his brother slantways, Gus said, "You kind of like that daughter of his too, don't you?"

Dolph grinned as he protested, "I ain't the one who was rolling around on the ground with her when I brought the ponies in."

"No, you were too busy letting the ponies stampede."

"That wasn't my fault. They spooked. Dammit, Gus, I don't know what the hell spooked them that way."

"I got a notion it was Eli or Edward, or the two of them," Gus said.

Dolph thought about it and nodded in agreement. He looked slantways at Gus. "Hey, if they tried to kill you once, they might try again!"

"I reckon they might."

"I don't think Ma would like it much if I was to come home without you. Likely she'd give me hell for losing you."

"Likely. Only I don't expect you to go home without me."

"You'd better keep a sharp eye on Edward and Eli."

"I figure to do more than that," Gus said. "You know Eli has a notion to convince everybody I'm the one who shot Boswick?"

"Yeah. Only he can't, on account of you didn't."

"Don't be too sure he can't. There's more than one man who got a free ride to heaven on a mistake. I'm going to be looking sharp all right, little brother. I'm going to be looking to find out just what's going on around here. Maybe by the time that lawman gets here, we can have the straight of it for him."

"You reckon so?"

"We can try. Brother, if any of these hairpins around here gets a hankering to talk, you listen. See if you can hear about any recent falling out between Edward and his pa. See what you can find out about Eli. He acts like he's a boss horse around here."

"He is. I heard already that Edward is the foreman and Eli's his segundo."

"They act more like Eli's number one and Edward's the segundo. See if you can find out how long Eli's been here and where he came from. Things like that. Be careful, though. Don't let Eli know you're interested in him. And keep your ears cocked behind you. If they're of a mind to shoot me, they might feel the same way about you."

"You think so?" Dolph seemed uncertain whether to be scared or pleased. Nobody had ever been after his hide before. The notion excited him.

"You just be real careful," Gus told him. "Ma would give *me* hell if I got home without *you*."

"Uh huh."

"Why don't you go over to the cookshack and see if the coosie's at work. Generally a coosie knows everything that's going on around a place."

"Generally a coosie is an ornery old cuss who won't waste a long look on a stranger."

"Generally a coosie is a man with a wreck box full of dirty dishes, or a woodbox waiting to be filled, or corn to be shucked, or taters to be skinned, or some kind of chores he'd be real happy to have a hand with," Gus answered. "Generally a real helpful stranger can cozy up to a coosie if he puts his mind to it."

"Hell," Dolph muttered under his breath. But he slid down from the corral rail and started toward the cookshack.

Gus licked his lips thoughtfully as he watched his brother walk away. He was more worried about Dolph than about himself. He had been in tight spots before. He figured he could take care of himself. Dolph was still young and green. But, hell, Dolph was man enough to be trusted off a tether.

There were riders coming toward the ranch house. He

turned to watch them. One was a ranch hand, the other
a bearded man in a dark suit. Likely the doctor, Gus figured. As the two of them approached the house, ranch
hands began to bunch up at the gallery. Eli came out of
the house, saw the riders, and called for them to hurry.

They came in at a gallop. As they reined up, the one
in the suit was already unlashing a black satchel from
the cantle of his saddle. Dropping off his horse, carrying
the satchel, he hurried into the house. Eli followed him.
The rest of the men waited, murmuring among themselves. Their voices were soft, subdued with worrying
and wondering.

Gus was worrying and wondering himself. It was important to him, to the family, that Boswick recover. But
there was nothing he could do about that. Nothing but
wait and hope.

"Hey, brother!" Dolph called as he came ambling up
to Gus. He was holding out both hands. There was a
slice of pie in each. He took a bite from one and offered
the other to Gus. Through a mouthful of pie he told
Gus, "The coosie wasn't there. Nobody around the
cookshack at all. Or at the bunkhouse either."

Gus sampled the pie Dolph gave him. It was dried apple, flavored with cinnamon and nutmeg. But it was tart.
Downright sour. Still, it was better than nothing. He
swallowed and told Dolph, "Likely the coosie's over at
the house with everybody else. The doctor got here.
He's inside with Boswick now."

One of the men by the gallery glanced toward Gus
and Dolph. He nudged the man next to him and whispered something. The second man looked up. Scowling,
he broke away from the bunch and strode toward Gus
and Dolph.

He was well past middle age, thin-shouldered and
heavy-hipped. As he approached, he glared at Gus. At
the piece of pie Gus was eating.

Gus guessed he was the *cocinero*. Nodding at the
man, Gus said pleasantly, "Morning."

"Where'd you get that pie?" the coosie growled at him.

Dolph hooked a thumb toward the cookshack. "I got it yonder."

"Who gave it to you?"

"Wasn't anybody there to give it to me. I had to take it for myself."

"You stole it!"

Dolph said, "It just smelled so good and looked so lonesome I had to take some."

"We were on the trail a long time with nothing to eat but our own cooking," Gus put in. "We got awful tired of wild greens and scorched game. We sure been looking forward to having something different."

"This is real different," Dolph added. "Not at all like our ma makes."

"You've got a mother?" the coosie grunted.

"Sure. Ain't everybody?"

"Not these buzzards around here! Every blasted one of them hatched out of a dungheap. Not a manjack among them knows decent food when he gets it. Nothing but catsup and chili and molasses. That's all they know. That pie sweet enough for you?"

Gus took a bite and rolled it on his tongue. He thought a dollop of long sweetening would help a lot. But he didn't want to rankle the coosie. "Mister, one damned drop of molasses would change the taste. This here is the taste it's supposed to have, ain't it?"

"It is! It damned sure is!" the coosie said, his scowl turning into a semblance of a smile. "You want more? You just come on over to the cookshack and get it."

"I'm obliged," Gus answered. "I'll sure be there later."

The coosie's face turned solemn. Speaking softly, he said, "Mister, if I was you, I wouldn't hang around here until later."

"How come?"

"Eli Tyler ain't got a lot of love for you. You've seen that for yourself, ain't you?"

Gus nodded. "Why you reckon that is?"

"Can't tell," the coosie said with a shrug. "Can't tell much about Eli any more. He ain't the same man he was a month or two ago. He's been going sour like something's ruining his bile. I'd say his liver's giving out on him."

"You think so?"

"That's what I'd say. He used to be decent enough. Hard but fair. Now he's as ornery as an old broody hen. There ain't but two things will do that to a man. Losing his liver or losing his woman."

"How you know he ain't lost his woman?"

"Hell, you can't keep a thing like that secret around a bunkhouse. It's his liver. Too much catsup and chili and molasses. Them things will corrode a man's liver every time."

"Hey!" Dolph gave a nod toward the house. "Is that the doctor?"

"Sure is," the coosie grunted. He dashed back to the gallery.

The doctor's voice carried clearly to the corral. "Men, I am pleased to announce that Mister Harry Boswick is resting comfortably. I have removed the bullet and the wound is clean. I've given him a sleeping powder and given Miss Vicky full instructions for his care. He has every prospect of a total recovery."

Eli had followed the doctor out onto the gallery. He stood waiting until the doctor had mounted up and ridden off. Then he shouted at the men, "Hell, ain't none of you got anything better to do than stand around here?"

At that the bunch broke, men heading off to their chores. Eli stalked down from the gallery. He seemed to purposefully avoid looking at Gus and Dolph as he passed them on his way to the barn. He went inside. After a few minutes he came out leading a saddled horse. He called to two men working nearby. He spoke briefly to them, then stepped to his saddle and galloped away.

"Where you reckon he's off to?" Dolph said.

Sliding down from the rail, Gus answered, "That's what I figure to find out."

"Catch me a horse and I'll go with you."

"No. You stay here and keep an eye on things. Edward should still be inside the house. If he comes out, you keep track of where he goes, who he talks to. If he rides off, you follow him. And watch them two there." Gus indicated the men Eli had spoken to. "I think they're supposed to keep an eye on us. Don't let them follow me."

6

Eli wasn't expecting to be trailed. He rode at a gallop, never looking back. Gus followed at a distance, staying just close enough to catch glimpses of Eli. He checked his own back trail. No one seemed to be after him. He hoped Dolph hadn't had any trouble with those two ranch hands. But Dolph was good at spinning windies that could confuse hell out of a man. He should be able to stall them off without getting himself hurt.

Eli kept to the road until he was within sight of the town at the end of the valley. It wasn't much of a town, just a cluster of buildings lining the road and a few houses scattered around on the slopes nearby. Slowing to a walk, Eli turned off the road and followed a pair of wheel ruts toward a small house.

There were woods near the road. Gus reined toward them. Finding a vantage point, he halted. Hidden in the shadows under the trees, he watched Eli draw up at the gallery of the house.

There was a dog lying on the gallery. It roused itself and gave a few gruff barks. It seemed to know Eli. As he climbed to the gallery, it met him. He patted its head, then knocked at the door.

Gus couldn't see the person who opened the door. He watched Eli step inside. The door closed. The dog looked at it a moment, then settled down.

Eli didn't stay long. When he left, he turned uproad, back toward the ranch. Gus stayed in the woods, letting him get well out of sight. Then he ambled his mount to

62

the road. At the point where the wheel ruts branched off, he halted and looked at the house.

It was a plain plank building, just big enough to have a couple of rooms on the first floor and a couple more upstairs. A one-story addition had been built onto one end, and the gallery extended to serve it. The addition had its own door. Next to the door a faded sign read GUNS—BOUGHT—SOLD—REPAIRED. J. G. NILES, GUNSMITH.

Gus touched the butt of the broken revolver at his side. Luck had funny ways of running. It seemed like bad luck when the gun busted on him. Now it was good luck, giving him an excuse to call at the house. Lifting rein, he rode up the wheel ruts.

The dog on the gallery rose to face him as he approached. It was a big animal, looking like close kin to a wolf. As he neared the house, it began to bark. It sounded serious. By the time he drew rein in front of the gallery, the dog was on the steps, showing him its teeth and giving him fair warning that it was willing to use them.

His horse snorted nervously, shaking its head and rattling the bit chain. Gus agreed. Staying in the saddle, he called to the house.

The door opened. A woman came out onto the gallery.

She was a handsome woman, mature but still well in her prime. She stood tall, and where her dress showed her figure, the curves looked full and soft. Her eyes were dark, deep, long-lashed. Lovely eyes. Except that they were reddened with crying. There was a catch in her voice as she spoke to the dog.

"Down, Rex. Sit."

The dog stopped barking. Moving to her side, it sat down and gazed warily at Gus.

"Afternoon, ma'am," Gus said, touching his hat brim to her. "That's a fine-looking dog you got there."

"He bites," she said. And she waited for him to tell her what he wanted.

"Is Mister Niles to home?" he asked.

She shook her head slowly. "Is it about a gun?"

"Yes, ma'am." He touched the Leech & Rigdon on his hip. "The hammer spring busted on me. You reckon Mister Niles could fix it for me?".

"Let me see it," she said.

He slid out of the saddle and started up the steps to the gallery. The dog growled at him. The woman put her hand on its head and it eased back.

"Good watchdog," Gus commented, holding the revolver out to her.

"Yes. He was the gift of a friend. A dear friend. He can kill a man," she said. "He'll attack on command."

Gus understood she was warning him to behave himself or she'd set the dog onto him. Glancing at the dog's bared teeth, he nodded.

She took the revolver from him and looked closely at it. "This isn't from the Colt factory. It's a Confederate imitation."

"Yes, ma'am. You know guns?"

She felt the loose hammer with her thumb. "I repair them."

Surprised, he said, "You ain't J. G. Niles?"

"I'm Dora Niles. Jim was my husband."

Gus eyed her curiously. He wondered if a woman really could repair a gun. "I never ran into a lady gunsmith before."

"When my husband was alive I helped him with his work. When he was taken ill I did the work under his direction. By the time he died, I knew the trade well enough to follow it. I guarantee my work. If it isn't satisfactory, I'll replace the gun to you at no charge," she told him.

He studied her face. She had been crying hard just moments ago. Now she was holding back the tears, standing firm and strong in front of a stranger. She defied him to doubt her ability. He had a feeling she was the kind of woman who really could do whatever she claimed. He said, "I'd be obliged to get it fixed as quick as I can."

She looked at the gun again. "These Confederate guns never were as carefully machined as Colt's revolvers. I doubt if I have a spring that will fit it. I'll probably have to adapt something to fit it. Do you have to have it back today?"

"I'd sure like it today, only I can't pay for the job right now," he admitted.

She lifted a brow at him, looking as if she expected him to ask for credit and then disappear without ever paying.

He resented that. "I got money coming. I might get hold of it tomorrow. I ain't sure. Thing is, I just drove a herd of ponies up to the Boswick ranch. I was supposed to get paid for them tomorrow. But there was trouble at the ranch. Now I'm not sure how soon I'll get my money."

He was watching her eyes as he spoke. He saw the flicker of interest at the name *Boswick*. It was more than casual interest, he thought. She had a strong, deep feeling for Harry Boswick. That was why Eli had come here. He'd come to tell her about the shooting. That was why she had been crying.

Wanting to know more, he asked, "You know Mister Harry Boswick, ma'am?"

"Yes." She sounded far away, as if her thoughts had gone off in a private direction.

"You heard about the trouble?"

She nodded. "Someone tried to murder Harry."

He felt an urge to comfort her. It was a strong urge. His hands wanted to touch her, to draw her close and stroke away her sorrow. He said, "No, ma'am. That shot wasn't meant for him. It was meant for me."

With a distracted shake of her head, she murmured, "They want to kill him because of me."

He started. Frowning, he said, "Ma'am?"

She was about to cry again. She didn't want to do it in

front of a stranger. Struggling to keep her dignity, she turned away from him. Her back to him, she said, "Please go away."

It might have been the decent thing to do, to leave her to cry in private. But Gus had questions. And he thought she might have some answers. Gently he said, "Ma'am, you're wrong. That bullet was meant for me, not for Mister Boswick. I'm sure of it."

She considered his words. Turning, she faced him again. "Why?"

"On account of a studhorse," he said, and he went on to tell her about the two men leading Caesar through the night. He explained how Boswick had moved suddenly into the path of the bullet. He told her, "I figure the men who were stealing the horse have a notion now that I can identify them. They didn't want me telling Boswick who they were. That's why they meant to shoot me. It was just an accident that he got hit."

She stared at him as if a thousand confused thoughts tumbled through her mind. She made no sound, but tears trickled down her cheeks.

"Ma'am," he suggested. "What you need is a good stiff drink. If you've got something in the house, I'll be glad to fetch it for you."

She gazed at him. He thought she could read the sympathy in his eyes. He thought she understood that he sincerely wanted to help. He hoped she wouldn't see that he had other reasons as well.

"It's in the kitchen,'" she said. Turning, she went into the house.

He followed her in. The dog growled, but it didn't move to stop him. She made no objection to his following her. They went through a small parlor into a neat, cheerful kitchen.

There was a bottle on the table, and a half-empty glass next to it. She had been drinking already. Trying to drown those sorrows, Gus supposed. She took another glass from a cupboard and handed it to him. Then she sat down at the table.

Gus poured for himself, sat down across from her, and sampled the drink. It was a wine. A dry wine with a flavor too much like vinegar to suit his taste. He thought of the weak whisky Boswick had given him, and longed for a shot of honest Texas rotgut.

Dora Niles sipped her drink. Softly she said, "I really do care for him."

"Ma'am?"

She looked up at Gus. She frowned slightly as she collected her thoughts. Suddenly she said, "Could you?"

"Could I what, ma'am?"

"Identify the men who were stealing Caesar."

He couldn't see any advantage in lying about it. He shook his head. "No, ma'am."

She smiled slightly. "That's good."

"Why?"

"It might be dangerous for you if you could."

"I reckon it's kind of dangerous for me now," he said. "Leastways if I'm right about that bullet being meant for me instead of Mister Boswick. As long as the thieves *think* I might identify them, they'll likely be gunning for me."

That seemed to trouble her, as if it really mattered to her. She took another taste of her drink as she considered. Hopefully she said, "Perhaps not."

He didn't want to frighten her, or to add to her worries. He nodded as if he agreed.

She seemed to understand that his nod was meant to reassure her. She gave him that slight smile again. He answered with a small smile of his own.

Her smile faded. Her eyes moved away from his face. For a long, silent moment she gazed past him into her own thoughts. He wondered what those thoughts might be. Her expression was wistful, as if she saw bright hopes beyond her grasp, and searching, as if she hunted a way to reach those hopes.

He waited for her to break the silence in her own time.

She seemed to reach a decision. Focusing on his face

again, she said, "I don't believe you told me your name."

"Gus Widner."

"May I speak frankly, Mister Widner?"

"Yes, ma'am. Sure."

"You seem to be a gentle person, Mister Widner," she said. "A kind and thoughtful man."

He couldn't help grinning self-consciously at that.

"Are you married?" she asked.

The question startled him. He didn't think she was considering him as a possible husband. Or maybe she was. He supposed a lone widow woman would be inclined that way. The notion that she was impressed enough by him to come right out and ask flattered him. She was a hell of a handsome woman. A smart one, too. He glanced around at the kitchen that seemed well-used and well-kept. Likely she would make a good wife. She kept a house a man could be proud of.

Embarrassed by his own thoughts, he took a long drink of the sour wine before he answered, "No, ma'am."

"Have you ever been in love?"

"I've thought so a few times," he admitted. "Only it turned out I was wrong. It never lasted long enough to mean anything."

"You're very fortunate."

"Ma'am?"

"Love is a complicated thing. Sometimes I think it's a terrible thing. A curse on mankind."

She wasn't heading in the direction he had anticipated. He couldn't figure what she was getting at. He frowned and said, "Ma'am?"

"Love makes us do terrible things. We can't help it. It just happens. A person can't stop it from happening just because it's wrong."

"How can it be wrong?"

She drank again, and when she set down the glass her mouth was curved into a suggestion of a sad smile. "If one of the two people isn't free . . ."

She left it there.

Suddenly Gus understood. She was talking about herself and Harry Boswick. He felt a surge of disappointment. And then anger at himself for the fool notion she might have taken a fancy to him. Hell, he should have known better than that. As far as she was concerned, he was just a saddle tramp, a stranger who happened along when she needed a shoulder to cry on. He reminded himself that he had come here for a reason. He wanted to know more about Harry Boswick and the troubles at the ranch.

She had left a thought implied but unspoken. He said, "You mean he's married?"

She had been staring down into her glass. She looked up from under her brows at him. "You know?"

He didn't like himself for what he was doing, using her need for sympathy as a way to pry. But she did want a shoulder to cry on, and he did intend to respect her confidence. He really did care. He answered with a nod.

"But how—oh—of course, I don't suppose I'm hiding it very well."

"No need to hide it at all, ma'am," he said.

"We never meant for it to happen," she told him. "But Harry brought some guns here for me to work on and we got to talking and we—it—neither one of us could help it. We tried to fight it, but we couldn't. It just happened."

"Only there's a Missus Boswick in the way?"

"Yes."

"I thought—I kind of got the impression she was gone. Dead or something."

"Gone," she said.

He caught an implication in her tone. He put it into words. "You mean she left him?"

She nodded.

"On account of you?"

"On no! It wasn't that way. She—I don't know. It was bound to happen." The tears were there again, trickling down her cheeks, making ugly paths on that lovely face.

He wanted to wipe them away. Kiss them away. He told himself it was only his shoulder she wanted, not his whole being.

Suddenly she spoke again, with anger in her voice. "Their marriage was meaningless. It had been for years. I don't know if she ever really loved him or only wanted his money and position. He was very young then, when he was married to her. And she was a shallow, useless woman. She wasn't suited to him at all. He has a marvelous mind. He's forever exploring, studying, learning. He's an exciting, fascinating person to be with. She never understood him, or cared about the things that had meaning for him. All she wanted was finery and flattery. She hated it out here. She kept trying to make Harry leave the ranch and take her back to England. Her and that son of hers."

"Edward?" Gus asked.

Nodding, she went on, "That woman was making life miserable for Harry and ruining his son. Harry wanted to make a real man out of Edward, but she wanted to spoil the boy. Harry could insist on rearing Edward like a man, but he couldn't stop her from teaching him discontent. She was making life miserable for everyone. For herself as well. She refused to give Harry a divorce. He would have made a good settlement on her. She could have lived in comfort wherever she wanted to. But she refused."

"Why?"

"Louise Boswick is a mean, nasty, vindictive woman. When Harry asked for a divorce, she told him he had ruined her life wasting her best years here in this wilderness, and she meant to see his life wasted in the same miserable way."

It didn't quite make sense to Gus. He said, "Then she up and ran away on him?"

"She betrayed him. She ran away with a friend of his. An English gentleman with a title who was visiting the ranch. The two of them simply disappeared. She didn't even have the decency to leave Harry a letter."

He took a drink of the wine as he pondered what she was saying. "You got a notion she's the one behind the trouble at the ranch now?"

She nodded.

"Why?"

"Because of me!" Flinging herself up out of the chair, she wheeled to put her back to Gus. Tears were overwhelming her. She hid her face in her hands as she sobbed.

Gus rose and stepped to her side. Tentatively he put a comforting hand on her shoulder. She accepted it and turned toward him. Then she was against him, and his arms were around her as she pressed her face into his chest and let herself cry.

"Listen here," he said softly, wanting to ease her pain. "If Missus Boswick wants her husband to suffer, she isn't going to kill him. That would be putting an end to his suffering the easy way."

She pulled back from him and looked up into his face. "That's so, isn't it!"

He nodded. "Do you reckon she would have that Caesar horse stolen from him? Would that hurt him deep?"

"Stealing Caesar would be—be almost like stealing Vicky from Harry. Caesar isn't just any horse. He's from stock that's been in Harry's family for centuries. Harry hand-raised him. He loves Caesar like a child of his own. If something were to happen to Caesar, it would break Harry's heart.

"Uh huh," Gus muttered to himself as he sorted his own thoughts. If Dora was right and Louise Boswick wanted revenge against her husband, she might have hired Eli Tyler to do the dirty work for her. Or maybe Edward wanted to avenge his mother and Tyler was working for him.

In any case, revenge might start with something like stealing a pet horse, but it wouldn't stop there. It could go on to destroying other things Boswick really cared about.

And maybe Boswick really did care for Dora Niles.

Gus wondered just how much he should say to Dora. He didn't want to hurt or frighten her. But there was strength in her. He decided she could handle the truth.

"Ma'am, if somebody really does want to get at Harry Boswick and make him suffer, there's a chance they'd try to do it by hurting the people close to him."

Her eyes widened in comprehension. "You mean me?"

He nodded. "You shouldn't stay out here alone."

"I'm not alone. I have Rex. Harry gave me Rex for protection."

"You need somebody to look out for you who can handle a gun."

"I can handle a gun," she told him.

"That ain't enough. You need another person here. A man who knows how to face up to trouble when it comes along."

"If you really think—I could ask my brother to come stay with me for a while."

"You got a brother in these parts?"

"Yes." She gave him a confident smile. "If you've been at the ranch, you may have met him. He works for Harry. His name is Eli Tyler."

7

"Eli can protect me," Dora said.

Gus swallowed hard and stared at her. He wanted a drink. Not that weak sour wine but a real drink. Eli Tyler was her brother.

He didn't trust Eli Tyler. Not one damned bit. And blood wasn't always a strong bond. Not every family was like his own. From the beginning, from Abel and Cain, there had been kinfolk who could turn on each other as easily as they turned against strangers.

He asked Dora, "Are you and him real close?"

"He's a good man." She sounded oddly as if she were arguing against an accusation. "He's been more than just a brother to me. Daddy died when we were just children. I was only a baby. Eli is almost ten years older than I am, but he was a child himself then. He had to quit school and go to work. Momma was sickly and she couldn't do much to support us. Eli had to be the head of the family. He kept us going. Even after Momma died, he took care of me just like a father."

There was a strange quirk in her smile. A hint of bitterness mingling with her fond recollections.

"Just like a father," Gus repeated after her, hoping she would say something more that would help explain her curious smile.

She nodded. "When I got old enough to understand how things were, I wanted to quit school and help him support us. That was before Momma died. Eli wouldn't let me do it. He insisted that education was important. He wanted an education himself. He was very ambitious. When he had the time, he'd sit down with me and ask me to teach him the things I was learning in school. He kept me at it, made me study and graduate with honors. Then later, after Momma was gone, I met Jim Niles and we fell in love. I thought that would make Eli happy. I thought it would be a relief to him to have me married. But he refused to give us his permission. He said Jim wasn't good enough for me. He always wanted the very best for me. Yes, Eli was like a father to me."

Like a very stern father, Gus thought. He said, "You went against him and married Jim Niles anyway?"

"We eloped," she admitted, sounding shy about it. "I thought that once I was gone Eli would see that it was best for all of us. But he tracked us down. There was a terrible row. I—he almost—but I stood by Jim, and finally Eli gave in. He was friendly after that and we kept in touch with each other, but I think—I don't think he ever really forgave me. Not until after Jim died. Then Eli came here to get me. He wanted to take me with him and take care of me. He said he'd find me another better husband than Jim."

Her voice caught in her throat. She paused, taking a deep breath, then went on, "Of course I couldn't do that. Eli had supported me for so long. I couldn't burden him with a widow to support for the rest of his life. And I knew that I could take care of myself. I insisted on staying here. That's when Eli found work at the ranch. He wanted to stay near me. To look out for me. He wanted to be close to me in case I needed him. He's really very sweet."

She was lying, Gus thought. But he had a notion she really believed her own lies. Sometimes people did that. Sometimes they bluffed themselves into accepting their own stories. She might claim Eli was a sweet, loving protector, but from the look of her eyes, Eli had really been downright possessive. Real possessive of his pretty baby sister, planning her life for her and resenting it when she tried to go her own way.

She was a strong woman. Eli couldn't have dominated

her easily. Just ordering her around wouldn't have worked. Eli must have used trickery on her, subtle lies and hints and maneuverings, to keep her thinking of him the way she did.

She had said Eli wanted to find her a better husband than Jim Niles had been. That was interesting. He asked her, "Were you and Harry Boswick—uh—friendly then? When Eli came here?"

"Before Jim died?" She was indignant at the implication. "Never! I had hardly even met Harry then."

"I didn't mean that," Gus protested, although it was exactly what he had been wondering. "I mean, did you know Boswick when he hired Eli? Did you help Eli get hired on at the ranch?"

"No." Her indignation eased away. "No, Jim had done work for him, and of course we all saw each other at church. I knew the Boswicks to say good morning to, but that was all. It was Eli who convinced Harry that I could handle his gun repairs after Jim died. There are men who wouldn't trust a woman to be a competent gunsmith, you know."

Gus nodded. He'd had that thought himself when Dora first took the broken revolver from him.

"Harry was wary of leaving me his work at first," she said. "But after we had talked a while, he decided to try it. He was satisfied with my work. And talking together the way we did, we kind of got to know each other. He kept coming back, bringing me more work and staying to talk a while about his own interests. Eventually I realized he was making work for me just as an excuse to come talk. After that we dropped the pretense and admitted the truth."

If Louise Boswick was really the kind of woman that Dora had described, Gus figured it must have been a real pleasure for Boswick to find a woman who shared his interests. From there on, the rest was inevitable.

He asked, "Was that very long ago?"

"About a year. It's just over two years since Jim died?"

"How long has it been since Missus Boswick ran off?"

"Not more than a month. Their visitor came just after the thaw floods began to go down. He stayed a few weeks. Long enough to—to get involved with *her*. Not long enough to really *know* her."

He frowned slightly. Someone else had spoken of something happening about a month ago. Yes, the coosie at the ranch said Eli Tyler began turning sour about a month ago. Could that have anything to do with Louise Boswick running away? That didn't fit the notion Gus had already formed. If Eli wanted a rich husband for his sister, he should have been happy to see Boswick's wife run off.

Maybe the coosie was wrong about Eli's liver. Maybe Eli had lost his woman. Maybe he had fancied Missus Boswick for himself, and then she had run away with another man.

But how could that connect with Eli and Edward stealing the studhorse?

"Hell," Gus muttered to himself.

Dora asked, "What?"

He shook his head. He had to know more than he did now if he was to make sense of whatever was going on around here. He looked at Dora, thinking of the possible danger to her. "I got to go back to the ranch, but I don't want to leave you here alone. Suppose you come on back with me. I expect you could put up there for a while."

"No." She shook her head. "It wouldn't be right. It wouldn't—I'd be—it wouldn't look right."

She had other reasons, Gus thought. He asked, "You think Edward and Miss Vicky wouldn't want you there?"

"Edward hates me," she admitted. "He was very close to his mother. He resents his father's interest in me."

"And Miss Vicky?"

"She's a sweet child. I think she would accept whatever is best for her father. But—" She shook her head again. "No, I couldn't go there. Not even to spend a few minutes at Harry's bedside. Not with Edward there."

"He don't mind Eli, though?" Gus asked.

"He doesn't know Eli is my brother. No one here knows, except you. I didn't intend to let anyone know. I hope you—please don't tell them."

"Don't worry, ma'am," he said. "Look, if you don't want to come to the ranch, is there somewhere else around here you could stay a while? Some folks who'll put you up for a few days without getting nosy about it?"

"I'll be all right alone. I have Rex."

"No, ma'am," he insisted. "You're not going to stay alone, you hear?"

He could see that she wasn't frightened for herself. She didn't really believe she was in danger. But she did appreciate his concern. Humoring him, she said, "I suppose I could stay with the Reverend Whatley and his family for a few days."

"All right," Gus agreed. "You go pack up whatever you'll need. Is that horse in the corral out back yours?"

"Yes. My buggy is in the shed."

"I'll hitch up for you."

Dora wanted to drive herself. She said it would be awkward trying to explain a strange man driving her to the Whatley house. Gus understood and agreed, but he rode at her side, escorting her most of the way. The dog trotted along behind, still casting wary glances at him.

When they caught sight of the house, Gus stopped. He waited, watching until he had seen her go inside. Then he turned back toward the ranch.

His thoughts kept drifting away from the puzzle of Eli Tyler. They insisted on turning to Dora Niles and his own feelings about her.

He envied Harry Boswick.

Riding past a point of woods into a broad meadow, he suddenly became aware of a rider on a ridge off to one side. Just as he looked toward the rider, he heard a shot. He saw the puff of smoke curling up from the rider's rifle.

The shot had been aimed in Gus's direction. But not at him. It was meant to get his attention. And maybe to warn him that the man with the gun was willing to fire again and place his next shot closer, if necessary.

Automatically Gus had started for the LeFaucheaux under his leg. He stopped his hand. Rising in his stirrups, he squinted at the rider. He thought he recognized the ranch hand, Ned.

With his rifle at his shoulder pointing toward Gus, Ned shouted. His voice carried the distance, but Gus couldn't make out the words. He got the impression Ned was threatening to shoot him, or some such damnfool thing. He was sure Ned didn't really want to kill a man. In reply, he lifted his hands out clear of his body, showing Ned that he didn't have a gun in either hand, or an intention of pulling one.

Ned lowered the rifle and kicked his horse into a gallop. Gus waited, holding rein on his mount, as Ned raced toward him.

Ned had the rifle ready as he halted in front of Gus. He looked Gus down, noting the hand with the reins resting on the saddle horn, the other hand open and palm up well away from Gus's body, and the LeFaucheaux still booted under Gus's leg. Some of the tension went out of him. He lowered the rifle.

"Where the hell did you get off to?" he asked.

"Why?"

"Eli's got every man who ain't on the range out hunting you."

"Why?"

Ned looked downright embarrassed as he admitted, "Eli's got a notion you shot Mister Harry somehow or another. He figures when you disappeared you were trying to get away ahead of the law."

"Why the devil would I shoot Mister Boswick? What do you think? You think I shot him?"

"Hell, I don't know. I don't see how you could have

done it, or why you would have. But Eli seems awful sure of it, and he's my boss."

And the boss is always right, Gus thought. He asked, "Does Eli want you to fetch me back to the ranch at gunpoint?"

"Uh huh."

"Or over my saddle?"

"Hell, I don't know!" Ned's eyes darted uncertainly to and from Gus's steady gaze. "I never been involved with nothing like this before!"

"It don't matter," Gus told him. "I'm heading back to the ranch now anyway."

Ned grinned in relief. As Gus lifted rein, he fell in alongside. After a moment he said, "I don't know what to make of Mister Harry getting shot that way. I can't figure who would do a thing like that."

"It wasn't me," Gus said. "Look here, if Eli has everybody off the ranch out looking for me, where's my brother?"

Ned shrugged. "Last I seen, Eli was talking to him."

"He ain't hurt him or locked him up or nothing?"

"Not that I know of."

"Does Eli really think I'd run off and leave my brother all alone there at the ranch with folks wanting to hang the two of us?"

Ned shrugged again. Sourly he said, "There ain't no telling what Eli thinks these days."

"Coosie says his liver's going bad," Gus commented. "Or else he's got woman trouble."

"I'd say woman trouble."

"How you figure that?"

Ned wasn't sure he should talk about it. But he wanted to. He admitted, "It's got to be something to do with Mister Harry's wife. I think Eli must have been moon-eyed over her. She ran off, and it was right after she left that Eli got to acting so funny."

Maybe Ned could supply some pieces to the puzzle. Gus kept his voice conversational as he asked, "What gives you the notion he was moon-eyed for her?"

"It's hard to say. I seen him looking at her a few times with a kind of funny look to his face." Ned frowned as he tried to put it into words. "Not exactly a moon-eyed look, but real thoughtful. You know. Like he was making plans of some kind in his head."

"You figure he was making plans about him and her?"

"I don't know, but—" Ned stopped himself short. "I don't reckon it's really none of your business."

"Maybe not," Gus allowed, giving Ned a friendly grin. "Only a man does get notions about a woman sometimes. And sometimes a woman will get notions about a man."

"Yeah," Ned said, grinning back at him. But the grin disappeared and Ned shook his head thoughtfully. "No, not Missus Boswick and Eli Tyler. She wouldn't get a notion for a poor dumb cowboy like him. If Eli ever spoke of such a thing to her, she'd have spit in his eye. Or maybe had his head lopped off like them old-timey kings of England in the school books. She wasn't the kind to say more than a good morning to a poor dumb dirty cowboy, and she wouldn't mean that."

"That so?" Gus said.

Ned didn't answer him. They had come within sight of the ranch house. The yard was empty. The place looked deserted. Rising in his stirrups, cupping his hands to his mouth, Ned gave a hoot.

Vicky Boswick came dashing out onto the gallery. She was clutching her skirts, almost running. She looked frantic. Spotting Gus, she shouted, "Mister Widner! Please hurry! Your brother! He's been hurt!"

Gus slapped spurs to his mount's sides. As he reached the gallery, he was jerking rein, dropping out of the saddle.

"What happened? Where is he?"

"In here." She gestured toward the house.

Gus took the steps two at a time. She held the door open for him. He rushed into the parlor and saw Dolph stretched out on a sofa.

There was a pillow under Dolph's head, and a trade blanket over him, pulled up to his chin. He lay still, his eyes closed. The flesh around them was swelling. His lips looked thick and pulpy. There was dried blood caked at the corner of his mouth. One hand was thrust from under the blanket. It lay palm up on a hassock that had been drawn close to the sofa. The fingers were curled. It looked like something that had rolled over and died there.

The breath caught in Gus's chest as he gazed at his brother. The anger, the fear, was a tight, cramping pain.

Vicky grabbed Dolph's limp hand in hers. As she clutched it, Gus saw Dolph's fingers tighten on the girl's small hand. He saw Dolph's lashes flutter slightly, and knew the eyes behind those lashes were watching him. A corner of Dolph's mouth quivered.

The breath went out of Gus in a sigh of relief. But he kept his face straight. Sounding disgusted, he grunted, "Hell, I thought you said he was *hurt*."

Vicky's eyes widened in surprise. Shock. She was appalled that Gus could seem so callous toward his brother.

"Brother," Gus said to Dolph. "You et yet?"

Dolph's battered lips twitched as he fought a grin. He couldn't hold it back. To cover it, he gave a small groan and slowly raised his eyelids. They were too swollen to open fully, but the pupils under them were bright with amusement. He turned his groan into a feeble *no*.

Gus looked at Vicky. Both brows lifted, his face blankly innocent, he said, "That's the trouble. It's way past nooning. He always gets like this when he misses a meal."

Dolph tried to hold back a sputtering laugh. He almost choked on it. Wheeling, Vicky dropped to her knees at his side. Her hands sought to comfort him. "Oh! Oh, you poor boy!"

Gus had more luck with his own urge to laugh. His face was still blank as Vicky demanded of him, "Can't you see how badly he's hurt? He may be dying!"

Dolph sounded like he might be dying. He was still choking on his own laughter. Gasping for breath, he managed to mutter faintly, "Water! Please!"

"I'll get it!" Vicky let go his hand and hurried to the kitchen.

As soon as she was beyond the door, Gus said softly to Dolph, "Brother?"

His tone said what the word didn't. It spoke sincere concern. And teasing accusation.

In reply, Dolph let his grin spread across his face. His voice was hoarse, but there was none of the weakness in it that had been in his groan for water. "She's sure something, ain't she?"

Gus grinned back at him. "What happened?"

"Eli. That's one hell of a feisty old bull."

"What happened?" Gus said again, wanting details.

"Brother, he beat the devil out of me. You think I'm not hurting, you ought to be where I am."

"You ain't hurt half as bad as you're putting on, and you know it. You've been marked up worse than that getting chucked off a green pony, and you've got on again and done a day's work."

"Uh huh," Dolph allowed. "But I don't like it any."

Small footsteps sounded beyond the kitchen door.

Sinking back onto his pillow, looking as sick as he could manage, Dolph whispered hurriedly, "Brother, please don't ruin this for me."

"Don't go getting no serious notions," Gus warned, recalling the things Ned had said about Vicky's mother. He didn't reckon the daughter would be for the likes of some poor dumb dirty cowboy either. Likely she was showing Dolph the same sympathy she'd show a hurt dog.

Dolph barely had time to lift a questioning brow at Gus. Vicky was back with the water. As she approached the sofa, Dolph groaned again. She slid an arm under his head, gently propping him up. Holding the glass to his lips, she said, "Here. Now drink it slowly."

Carefully, as if small movements pained him, Dolph

put a hand to the glass. His fingers resting over Vicky's, he sipped at the water.

Gus didn't intend to come right out and ruin the game for Dolph, but he thought it wouldn't do any harm if he let Dolph squirm a bit. Solemnly he said, "Has the doctor seen him yet?"

The last thing Dolph wanted was a doctor. Reproach flashed in his eyes.

Vicky's eyes were tender with concern. "I was going to send someone, but I couldn't find anyone. There's not a hand on the place. Maria's at Father's side. I couldn't send her. I thought I might go myself, but I didn't want to leave him alone. I wasn't sure what to do. Then I heard Ned call and—oh! I could send Ned!"

She started to her feet.

"No!" Dolph protested. He groped a hand toward Vicky. It found her skirt and grabbed on, like the hand of a desperate man clinging to his last straw. "Don't go! Don't leave me!"

"Of course I won't." She detached the hand from her skirt and clutched it in both of hers, caressing it as one might pet a small, frightened animal. To Gus she said, "You could go."

"No," Dolph repeated. "No, don't bother. I'll be all right."

"He don't like the idea of doctors," Gus said to Vicky. "We don't have them down home. We tend to hurt folk ourselves."

Dolph made a sound of agreement, and groaned, "I don't need any doctor."

"Are you sure?" Vicky asked him.

"Somebody ought to look over him, see if he's got any busted bones," Gus said.

"I'm all right," Dolph insisted.

"I reckon we could do it," Gus suggested.

Vicky blinked in confusion. She was upset that she hadn't thought about the possibility of broken bones herself. And uncertain what to do about it. She stammered, "I—can you—?"

"Sure." Gus eyed her slantways as he spoke. "You want to help me undress him?"

Her cheeks colored. She looked down at the glass of water that she still held, hiding her eyes from Gus. "I—do—can you do it alone? He's going to need nourishment. Maria put soup on to simmer a while ago. I'd better see if it's ready yet. You can look for the broken bones by yourself, can't you?"

Gus nodded.

Vicky gave Dolph's hand a squeeze. Embarrassed, she slipped out of the room. Gus figured she'd be gone for a while this time. She'd wait outside until she was certain he had finished examining his brother's body.

"All right, brother," he said, seating himself on the hassock at Dolph's side. "Tell me what happened."

8

Dolph squirmed around to prop himself on an elbow. As he did it, he grunted with pain. This time it was no performance to get sympathy. The grunt was unintentional, the pain real.

Frowning at him, Gus asked seriously, "You ain't got any broken bones, have you?"

"I don't think so," Dolph admitted as he wriggled himself comfortable. "Mostly he hit me in the face. With a shovel, I think. He just slammed it right into me. He did kick me a couple of good ones in the gut, but I don't think he busted anything."

"You're sure?"

"Uh huh."

"Did you get him back?"

"No, dammit!"

"Why not?"

"Like I said, he hit me with a shovel or something. He bushwhacked me. I never got a chance at him. I want him, brother. I want me a couple of good licks at him!"

"Sure, Gus agreed. "Likely you'll get them. Why did he jump you?"

"He had been asking me where you'd got off to, and I had been kind of ragging him. I guess it got his hackles up." Dolph paused thoughtfully. "I got a notion it was more than that though. It was like he was all primed and ready to explode. You know how a critter with a fighting nature gets when he's riled and he can't get hold of whatever he's mad at? Like a bobcat in a cage? You know how he'll go at whatever he can get hold of and he'll tear hell out of it? I think it was something like that with Eli. It was like he was taking a whole mess of mad out on me. Like he went kind of loco."

"I reckon he wanted me," Gus said. Remembering the look of deep desperation in Eli's eyes, he thought there was more to it than that.

"He sure wanted to know where the hell you went off to. Where did you go, brother?"

"I followed him."

"Where did he go?"

"To see a lady."

Dolph grinned. It was a questioning grin, with hints of insinuation in it.

"I reckon he came straight back here from there," Gus speculated.

"I reckon," Dolph said, looking slantways at Gus. "He wasn't gone very long. Not near as long as you were gone."

"I stopped off to see the lady, too."

"A pretty lady?"

"Damned pretty," Gus admitted. He flashed a grin back at Dolph, then asked. "Did you get friendly with the coosie like I said you should?"

"Uh huh. I went and helped him peel taters. I cut myself." Dolph held up his hand, showing a small, fresh cut among the scars on a calloused forefinger.

"Oh, you poor boy!" Gus mocked Vicky's sympathy.

Dolph scowled at him. "Don't you go making fun of her! Brother, that's one hell of a fine woman there."

"That's one hell of a rich woman there," Gus said.

"What's wrong with that?"

"She's an educated woman, brother, from a real fancy old family that's likely got a lot of pride in itself. She's a thoroughbred. You and me, we're mustangs. Plain old Texas cayuses. And you'd better not forget it."

"It don't make any difference!" Dolph protested. "Hell, our family's just as old and proud as anybody's!"

Gus could see that Dolph was serious enough to start

getting mad. There was no time for that now. No time for arguing about Vicky Boswick. Gus had to find out what he could about Eli Tyler before Vicky came back.

With a change of tone, picking up as if there had been no interruption in his line of thought, he asked, "Then what happened?"

Dolph hesitated, recalling where he had left off his story. He was still frowning at Gus as he went on, "I was peeling taters for the coosie and I went outside to fetch some water, and that's about when Eli showed up. He came stomping around wanting to know where you were. I said some damnfool thing or another, making fun of him, and got him huffed. He went hollering for the ranch hands to all saddle up and go hunt you. He kept saying you were the one who shot Boswick and you'd run off to escape a hanging."

"Did they believe him?"

"Not much, I don't think. They didn't act very het up. But they did what he told them. He was plenty het up, brother. He even sent the coosie off with them to look for you. I just hung around watching to see what he was up to. Once everybody had left, he started acting funny. He went sneaking into the barn. He made out like he was trying to keep me from seeing him, so I just naturally up and followed him."

"Naturally."

"Only he was just flagging me into a trap. When I sneaked in after him, he was waiting for me. He laid a shovel, or something like one, across my face. It flattened me out. He whacked me with it a couple more times and then kicked me a couple of times, and that's about all I remember of it." Dolph grinned as if the whole thing amused him.

Gus lifted a brow. "That's your idea of fun?"

Dolph kept on grinning. "What came afterward is."

"You mean moaning to Miss Vicky and having her hold your hand and all that?"

"I didn't go moaning to her. She saw me stagger out of the barn, and she came running to help me. Brother, she was all sweet and sorry for me, and I couldn't let it go to waste, could I?"

"Did you tell her what happened?"

"Un ugh. I didn't reckon it would be a good idea, so I've been way too sick to do any talking. I've been way too sick for much of anything except holding her hand."

"Yeah." Gus couldn't help grinning a bit. He didn't blame Dolph. He supposed he would have done the same in Dolph's place. Vicky was sweet and pretty, and it would likely be a lot of fun to hold her hand a while. But he didn't expect a dirty cowboy could hope for more than that.

He wondered if he should keep trying to warn Dolph or let him learn his lesson the hard way. Hell, a man had to get hurt now and then. That was the way of things. He decided to let Dolph play out his own hand. He would go along with it. When Vicky got back, he'd let Dolph go on playing invalid. Meanwhile, he had to get the rest of Dolph's story.

"How about the coosie?" he asked. "You ain't told me whether you found out anything from him."

"I sure did. I found out something funny about when somebody tried to rob Boswick's safe. It seems like nobody could find horse sign or anything like that anywhere around the place."

"Like maybe it was somebody here at the ranch who was at the safe?"

"Uh huh."

"Find out anything else?"

"Yeah," Dolph said. "But I don't reckon it had anything to do with the trouble here now."

"What's that?" Gus asked.

"Boswick's wife ran off from him a few weeks ago. She ran off with another man."

"I found that out myself."

Dolph looked disappointed that his news wasn't news. But he had more to add. "The funny thing is that all the ranch hands figured this hairpin had his eyes on Miss Vicky. Nobody thought he ever looked twice at Missus

Boswick until he up and disappeared with her. It was real sudden."

"Do you know whether that was before or after somebody tried to rob the safe?"

"Before, I think. From what the coosie said, I reckon it was a week or so before. You figure they had something to do with the robbery?"

Gus shrugged. "It could be they hung around looking to get hold of a mess of money."

Dolph caught the doubt in Gus's voice and said, "You don't really think that."

"No. It don't seem likely. From what I heard, the man she ran off with was another fancy Englishman like Boswick. I expect he had plenty of money already. It seems to me more likely it was Eli or Edward trying to get into the safe. Maybe both of them, like they tried to steal that studhorse together."

Dolph nodded in agreement. But he asked, "Why would Edward want to steal from his own pa?"

"From what I've heard, he works for a wage. His pa doesn't share anything with him. And he ain't happy that—" Gus stopped short. Cocking an ear toward the door, he held up a hand for silence.

He could hear someone coming up the steps to the gallery. Someone wearing heavy boots and spurs. He rose and went to the door. He waited until the man outside knocked. Then he swung the door open.

Eli Tyler stood there with his hat in one hand. The other hand dangled close to the butt of his revolver. He wasn't surprised to see Gus. But then Ned had probably told him Gus was there.

For an instant he glowered at Gus. Then, glancing into the parlor, he said, "Where's Miss Vicky?"

Gus felt an urge to mark Eli the way Eli had marked Dolph. But this wasn't the time or the place. He kept his voice soft and his anger under a tight rein. "In the kitchen."

"Where've you been?" Eli demanded. He, too, kept his voice low, as if he didn't want it to carry as far as the kitchen and Vicky. "You weren't supposed to leave the ranch."

Instead of using his fist, Gus hit Eli with words. "I went to see your sister."

The muscles of Eli's face tightened. The color drained away in harsh anger. "My sister! What the hell business you got seeing my sister!"

He shoved toward Gus as he spoke. Gus backstepped, letting him force his way into the parlor.

At the knock, Dolph had slumped down onto his pillow, reassuming his role as a badly injured man. When he saw Eli he had a strong urge to attack. But he realized that if he did it here and now, he would give himself away to Vicky. She would know he had only been putting on a show of pain. Keeping her sympathy seemed to mean more to him right now than taking revenge on Eli. Watching from under lowered lids, he told himself he would get his chance later. And besides, he wanted to know how Gus would answer Eli's question.

Gus grinned at Eli. It was an ugly, calculated grin.

"What the hell did you go to my sister for?" Eli said, forgetting to keep his voice down.

Vicky heard him. From beyond a closed door, she called, "Eli? Is that you?"

Eli sucked breath. His eyes darted as if he had suddenly discovered himself in a trap. He scowled at Gus, silently telling him that he meant to deal with him later. To Vicky he called back, "Yes, ma'am."

"Is it all right for me to come in now?" she asked.

"Yes, ma'am," Gus called before Eli could reply. "You come right on in."

As she opened the door, Eli pulled himself under control. His face still pale, still stiff, he nodded to her in greeting.

She gave him only a glance as she hurried to Dolph's side. She grabbed up Dolph's hand in hers. With most of her attention on Dolph, she said to Eli, "I'm so glad you're here. Do you have any idea what could have happened to this poor boy?"

His eyes narrow and wary, Eli asked, "He didn't tell you?"

She shook her head. "He's barely conscious. He hasn't been able to talk. I was hoping you might know. Oh, Eli, something terrible is happening here!"

"Yes, ma'am," Eli muttered. He was watching Gus. Gus was grinning at him like a bobcat smiling at a rat it had under its claws.

Gus guessed that Eli had plans, and taking his temper out on Dolph could have hurt those plans. Eli looked relieved that Vicky didn't know what went on in the barn. Gus wondered if she should be told. He decided against it. She had worries enough with her father injured and her mother gone, and strange things happening around her.

He said, "Maybe a horse stomped him."

"Do you think so?" she asked. She seemed hopeful, but doubtful that he was right.

He shrugged.

Eli eyed him suspiciously, knowing he should be able to tell the marks of a beating from those of a stomping.

Gus was standing aside from Vicky, a little way ahead of her. She couldn't see his face. He grinned at Eli again, in that bobcat way.

Trying to ignore him, Eli said to Vicky, "Ma'am, would you know where Edward is?"

She sounded embarrassed as she said, "He left the house at least an hour ago. He was—I think he may have gone to town."

"Yes, ma'am." Eli's tone was sympathetic, as if he understood her embarrassment. "Maybe I ought to go after him."

"Please do," she said appreciatively.

Eli continued, as if he were pressing a point, "Maybe he'll need help getting home. Was he drinking before he left?"

She didn't want to admit it, but her tone allowed that he had been. "Please go after him."

"Yes, ma'am." Eli put his hat on his head and stalked out of the parlor.

Stepping to the door, Gus watched him. There was a saddled horse ready at the hitch rail. Eli swung on board. He glanced back as he loped toward the road. Seeing Gus watching, he put his horse into a gallop.

So Edward had gone to town to get drunk, Gus thought. He got the impression Edward had done that more than a few times before, and had got himself so roostered that he couldn't get home again under his own steam.

Eli was almost around the first point of woods that would hide him from sight, when the sudden sound of a gunshot snapped flat and harsh from the direction of the barn.

Gus flinched, and his hand went for the revolver that should have been at his side. But that gun was at Dora Niles' place. Wheeling, he ducked back into the house. There were several gun racks in the parlor, all of them full.

Vicky had turned toward the door. As he came through it, she asked, "What was that? It sounded like a shot."

He nodded. "Any of these guns loaded?"

Her eyes questioned him as she pointed toward a rack of long guns near the office door. He didn't answer. Snatching a rifle from the rack, he checked the action. She was right. It was loaded. He cocked it as he ran from the house toward the barn.

Over his shoulder, he glanced toward the woods. Eli should have heard that shot. But he hadn't come back. He was out of sight now.

Gus was glad of that. Whatever the hell was going on, at least Eli wouldn't be around to interfere for a while.

9

Gus was aware that Vicky had come out of the house and was hurrying after him. As he reached the corner of the barn, he stopped short. She came up behind him. He thrust out a hand to stop her, to gesture her back. She halted at his side.

For a moment he stood silent, holding his breath as he listened. There was stock in the barn. He could hear the nickering and restless shuffling, but that was all. No sounds of a man. He took a breath and scented smoke.

Just because he couldn't hear a man didn't mean there wasn't one. Someone could be waiting inside, ready to bushwhack anyone who stepped through the doorway.

"You get on back to the house and stay there," he whispered to Vicky. Cautiously he edged toward the open barn door.

She didn't obey but followed along behind him.

"Get back," he said again, quietly, through his teeth, making a stern order of it.

She stopped following him then, but she didn't go back. She stood watching as he grabbed a quick look into the barn.

A small fire was burning in the middle of the dirt floor. It was well away from anything it might catch and spread across. Next to it, a man lay on his belly. His face was toward the fire. His hands were outstretched. One held a revolver.

It could have been a trap like the one that Eli had lured Dolph into, but Gus didn't think so.

He heard the faint rustle of Vicky's skirts as she came up close behind him. He could hear her soft breaths, and her sudden gasp as she looked past him into the barn.

Cautiously, not wanting to believe her eyes, she said, "Edward?"

When she said it, Gus realized she was right. The dark figure in the shadows was her brother.

She started to push past Gus. He caught her with one arm, holding her back. "I don't think you ought to, ma'am."

"No!" she said. "He's only drunk! I've seen him like this before. I know what to do for him!"

She was lying to herself, Gus thought, and she knew it. Gently he said, "No, ma'am, not this time. You go on back to the house. I'll take care of him."

She hesitated. Slowly admitting the possibility to herself, she asked Gus, "Is he dead?"

The sunlight that fell through the barn door didn't reach the body on the ground, and the small fire cast only a faint flickering light. Even so, Gus was certain. The man on the ground had that look Gus had seen often on battlefields and occasionally in other places. Sometimes it was hard to tell just by looking. But sometimes there was a stiffness, a hollowness, a shriveled, shrunken look that the eyes couldn't miss. He had no doubt about it as he said, "Yes, ma'am."

She seemed to go cold and stiff, then limp against his arm. Her head swayed. For an instant he thought she was fainting. Then she tensed. Caught a breath. Looked up into his face. Her eyes glanced into his. She turned her head and pulled away from his arm. Standing without his support, breathing raggedly, she said, "I—I'll be all right."

He wasn't sure. She still looked as if she might keel over. But he knew he could only offer her protection. He couldn't force it on her. In the end she had to make her own decisions.

Nodding, he walked on into the barn. He didn't try to keep her from following him.

The fire had been small to begin with. Now it was burning low, about to gutter out. Setting down the rifle, he took a lantern from a wall peg. He used a piece of straw to take a flame from the fire for the candle inside the lantern. By its light he looked closely at the body.

The hole in Edward's upturned temple was small and puckered, darkened by the scorching of a muzzle flash very close to the skin. The pistol in the dead man's hand was one of the army model Colt revolvers, a .44 or .45 caliber. That surprised him. The shot he had heard hadn't sounded big enough for the gun.

Vicky dropped to her knees next to Edward, reaching out to take the dead man's head in her hands. Gus snatched her wrist. He gripped harder than he had meant to. She winced at the pain. Her eyes turned toward him, startled and suddenly frightened of him.

"You don't want to look," he told her. "You ought to be back to the house."

She shook her head.

"It'll be ugly," he warned. But the decision was hers. She nodded.

He let go her wrist. Gently, in respect for her, he turned the dead man over. The body rolled with an awkward stiffness. The eyes were open. They seemed to stare at Gus as the head turned up its hidden side.

Vicky gasped.

The big slug had gone through Edward's head. The hole it made coming out wasn't nearly so neat as the one it made going in.

Gus reached for Vicky's hand, meaning to comfort her if he could. He felt the chill in her fingers and saw the pallor in her face. With a small sobbing sound, she went limp.

This time she had fainted.

He gathered her in his arms. Rising, he turned toward the door.

Someone was coming.

Gus hesitated, glancing at the rifle he had left leaning against a stall gate. The unconscious girl filled his arms. He started to put her down and grab the gun.

"Gus?"

The voice that called was Dolph's. Recognizing it, Gus let out a sigh. He steadied the girl in his arms again as he answered, "In the barn, brother!"

Dolph came through the doorway carrying a shotgun from the rack in the parlor. He had it leveled, ready to be used if need be. It jerked in his hands as he saw Vicky.

"What the hell!" he gasped. "What happened?"

"She fainted," Gus said quietly. "You want to aim that thing somewhere else?"

"She ain't hurt or anything?"

"No. She only just fainted. She'll be all right. Put that thing down, will you?"

Dolph looked at the gun he held as if he hadn't known about it. It was pointing toward his brother, and Vicky. His face flushed as he lowered the twin muzzles.

"What happened?" he asked again, more calmly this time.

"I told her not to look but she did anyway." Gus gave a nod toward the body on the floor behind him. "That's Edward. He's dead. It ain't pretty."

"Dead?"

"Uh huh. It looks like he shot himself. In the head."

Dolph swallowed hard. He looked past Gus at the body, then at the girl in Gus's arms. Setting down the shotgun, he said, "Here, give her to me. I'll take care of her."

All that moaning and groaning in the parlor might have been playacting, Gus thought, but Dolph really did look a little sick, and wobbly on his feet. He asked, "You sure you can handle her?"

Dolph nodded. Determination showed in his face. If Vicky needed help, he meant to be the one who gave it to her. He reached out for her.

At his touch, she made a small sound. Startled by it,

he jerked back. Her eyes blinked open. They were glazed, unfocused and unseeing. Frightening.

Dolph had seen dead men before. Bodies didn't bother him. But he'd had small experience with fainted women. He asked cautiously, "Miss Vicky? Are you all right?"

Suddenly she squirmed in Gus's arms and gasped, "Put me down!"

"We're taking you back to the house," Gus told her.

Her squirming turned into a frantic struggle, as if she were terrified of him. "Don't touch me! Put me down!"

"You're scaring her, Gus," Dolph snapped. "Let her go!"

She was too upset to be carried. Gus lowered her feet to the ground. Even as he opened his arms, she was fighting to escape them.

Dolph held out a hand, meaning to comfort her. She jerked back, away from him. She almost stumbled. Catching her balance, she kept backing until she had come up against a stall gate. There, she pressed herself against the gate as if she hoped to melt into it.

Dolph held both hands out toward her, but he didn't try to touch her. Soothingly he said, "It's all right, Miss Vicky. It'll be all right."

She shook her head as if in denial. For a moment she was staring at him like a cornered animal. Slowly she steadied herself. She brushed a hand across her face. Her forehead was wet with perspiration. She wiped at it.

"Here." Dolph held his bandana out to her.

She didn't seem to see it. Her gaze was inturned and uncertain. Fighting her panic, she said, "I—did I faint?"

"Yes, ma'am," Gus answered.

She turned to Dolph then and looked at him as if she had just discovered his presence. "Oh. But you shouldn't be up. You're hurt. You should be resting."

"I'm fine," he said, embarrassed by the admission but wanting to reassure her. "I was worried about you."

"You're hurt," she repeated insistently. There was a vagueness in her voice that Gus didn't like. She seemed on the bare edge of self-control, close to slipping away. She might faint again. Or worse. She could lose that control completely and never get it back again.

"Yes, ma'am, he's hurt bad," he said, wanting to distract her from thoughts of her dead brother. "You better take him back to the house and look after him. He needs you."

She nodded.

Dolph missed the point. He grunted, "Hell, I'm all right."

Gus darted a glowering look at him, hoping he would understand, or at least recognize an order and obey it. But all of Dolph's attention was on Vicky.

"Ma'am, don't you worry," Dolph was saying. "It will be all right. You let me take you back to the house now."

Frowning, she shook her head. She looked puzzled. "There was something I—oh! *Edward!*"

Suddenly she was crying. She turned away, covering her face with her hands, pressing her forehead to the stall gate.

Dolph started toward her as if he meant to grab her into his arms. Catching him by the shoulder, Gus held him back and whispered, "Don't! You'll only scare her again. Let her cry it out. She'll be better afterward."

Dolph looked doubtful. But Gus was certain the tears were the healthy kind that would ease the pressures within her. With a nod, he pulled Dolph away from her.

As he moved, something caught his eye. To himself he muttered, "What's that?"

"What?" Dolph asked.

"That." Gus stepped over to the dead man. Hunkering, he picked up a folded piece of paper. It had been under Edward's body, hidden by it before Gus turned the body over. He thumbed open the folds.

Lines of letters like the printing in a newspaper marched across the sheet. It was a note that had been made on the pterotype writing machine in Boswick's office. Gus held it close to the lantern. His lips moved slightly as he read the words to himself.

I killed Mama and her lover and hid the bodies where you will never find them. Edward.

"Damn!" he grunted.

Suddenly he was aware of a presence behind him. Vicky was no longer crying. She was standing there, reading the note over his shoulder.

"No!" she gasped. "He didn't! He couldn't have!"

Her tone startled him. It wasn't the kind of denial that came only from hope. It sounded like she had some sure knowledge.

He asked, "How do you know?"

"Because *I*—" she stopped herself. Her eyes had that trapped animal look. Weakly she said, "I know Edward. He wouldn't. He couldn't."

"You know more than that," he said.

"No!" She shook her head insistently. "No!"

Dolph had been hunkering at Gus's side, reading the note along with him. When Vicky spoke, Dolph rose and wheeled toward her. He put a hand on her arm. She shuddered at his touch, and he drew the hand back again. He stood poised, looking into her face. She was staring at Gus as if she saw some terrible threat in him.

Dolph wanted desperately to help her. He said to Gus, "Leave her alone."

Gus would have preferred to leave her alone. He didn't want to hurt her, or drive her any deeper into the panic he could see behind her eyes. But she knew something about this mess. She had some important secret that he needed to know to understand what was happening on the ranch. He had to understand it, to have facts for the lawman who was coming. He had to be able to clear himself and his brother of the accusations being made against them.

The more self-control she regained, the less likely she was to admit her secret. He had to pressure her now if he hoped to learn it.

Hating what he had to do, he rose to face her. He grabbed her wrist. She flinched. Holding tight, he insisted, "What do you know about it?"

"Nothing!"

"Gus!" Dolph snapped. "Leave her alone!"

Dolph's tone surprised Gus. It startled him enough that he eased his grip on Vicky's wrist. Dolph had disagreed with him in the past, and had disputed him more than a few times, but he had never actually gone against him. Now there was outright challenge in Dolph's voice. He was giving an order, making a demand.

It wasn't easy for Dolph to oppose his older brother, the brother he'd been taught all his life to respect and obey. But he ached in sympathy for Vicky. A little apologetic, but still defiant, he said, "You were hurting her."

"She knows something about all this," Gus said.

"No," Vicky protested. Gus's fingers circled her wrist loosely now. She jerked her hand away and moved toward Dolph. Toward his protection. She sidled up to him, and he put a hand on her arm, she didn't draw away.

"I won't let anybody hurt you," Dolph told her.

"I don't want to *hurt* her," Gus said. He didn't want to hurt Dolph either. This whole business was going against his grain. He hated pressuring the girl. He'd only done it because he felt he had to. Now he felt almost relieved that it was too late to go on. She was collecting herself, using Dolph as a shield. She wouldn't answer him now, not with Dolph at her side that way.

She spoke to Dolph, "Please take me back to the house."

"Sure," he said, starting to turn with her.

Gus looked at Edward's body again. And at the ashes of the little fire. Dropping to one knee, he poked at the ashes.

Dolph saw him and paused. "What are you doing?"

"That fire wasn't set to burn the barn down," he said. "It was set to burn up something smaller. Something maybe it didn't burn up completely."

Fear flashed in Vicky's eyes. She made no move to go on to the house, but stood at Dolph's side, clinging to his hand, as she watched Gus prod at the ashes.

He found something and nudged it out with a finger-tip. It was still hot. Picking it up, he juggled it in the palm of a calloused hand.

Cautiously, needing to know, but afraid of knowing, Vicky asked, "What is it?"

"A pistol ball." Gus held it out for her to see. It was as round as if it had just come from the mold. Not a trace of a scar from slamming through a gun barrel marred it.

Vicky frowned at in puzzlement.

Dolph asked, "What about it?"

"You recollect that shot we heard?" Gus said. "You recollect how it sounded? Kind of flat?"

Dolph nodded uncertainly. He didn't really remember at all.

Gus said, "I don't think Edward killed himself."

Vicky's eyes widened. She didn't understand. The fear was in her face again.

"It looks to me like someone else shot Edward," Gus told her. "Like somebody else might have made that note on your pa's machine to make it look like Edward wrote it. Like there's a killer running loose around here."

Confused, she mumbled, "But I thought . . ."

When she didn't finish, Gus asked her, "Thought what?"

She was lost in the muddle in her own mind. From the depths of her confusion, she whispered faintly, "I thought he did it for me."

"For you?" Dolph asked her.

She nodded. Covering her face with her hands, she said through her fingers, "*I* killed Mama and Rod."

10

Vicky had her face pressed into her hands, but this time she wasn't crying. She seemed beyond tears. She just stood, looking limp, as if she were awaiting some doom she couldn't possibly escape.

If what she said was true, then Gus felt he could understand that deep sorrow he had seen in her eyes. But was it true? Certainly she hadn't murdered her brother, or written the note that Gus still held in his hand.

Suddenly he was aware of hoofbeats. Several horses were galloping into the yard, toward the barn. Dropping the note, he wheeled to snatch up the rifle he had brought from the house. He swung the muzzle toward the barn door.

Vicky heard the horses too. She jerked up her head and stared toward the door.

Dolph was standing at her side, so concerned for her that he hadn't noticed the hoofbeats. Her sudden move startled him.

She lunged forward. Grabbed up the note Gus had dropped. And flung herself toward the doorway. As she raced past Gus and on out into the yard, she screamed. It was a wild, terrified scream.

It triggered the men in the yard into a dash for the barn.

Vicky ran to meet them.

Gus scanned the men, then glanced down at the rifle he was holding. Meeting these men with a cocked gun might not be a good idea. Eli Tyler wasn't among them, and Eli was the one who wanted him dead. So far the rest of the hands hadn't accepted Eli's claim that Gus shot Boswick. Gus didn't want to antagonize them. He didn't want to give any of them any reason to side with Eli. Waving the gun could cause trouble.

Taut, moving against an instinct to keep himself armed, he set the rifle down again.

There were four men outside. As they reached the barn, they slung themselves down from their saddles. One was the coosie. Vicky ran to him. Like a frightened child, she threw herself against him and pressed her face to his chest. Tentatively he patted her back.

The other three men had jerked out handguns as they came off their horses. They headed warily to the barn.

Gesturing for Dolph to join him, Gus met them in the doorway. He stood facing three drawn guns, feeling naked without a weapon of his own. But there was no trouble here, he insisted to himself.

"What is it?" one of the ranch hands demanded. "What the hell's going on?"

"It's Edward." Gus nodded toward the body in the barn. "He's dead."

Vicky flinched in the coosie's arms. Gasping for breath, she shouted, "They've murdered him!"

Aghast, the coosie glowered at Gus and Dolph. "Who? These two?"

Vicky hesitated. She lifted her head and looked at Gus and Dolph. For an instant her gaze met Dolph's. She blinked as she looked away. Slowly she gave a small nod.

"No," Dolph muttered, sounding puzzled and hurt.

"Hell, no!" Gus protested, puzzled himself. Why the devil would she tell a lie like that?

Clutching the coosie's hand in hers, Vicky mumbled, "Please—I want to go to my room."

"Yes, missy." The coosie patted her back again, and turned to walk her to the house. She hung heavily on his arm as if she were exhausted.

"Brother, what the hell is going on?" Dolph asked.

Gus shrugged. He glanced at the guns pointed toward

him, and wondered if he should have kept hold of that rifle. He decided not. He didn't want to shoot any of these men. If he'd had a gun in his hand, someone might have forced him to use it.

Quietly he said to the men facing him, "It's a mistake. Miss Vicky is wrong. Maybe she didn't understand. She's all upset. She didn't mean what she said."

"She meant it all right," one ranch hand said grimly. He was a tall man with a dark, pock-marked face. His eyes were narrowed and his jaw was clenched with anger. His revolver was leveled at Gus's gut. He looked as if he'd like to pull the trigger and be done with it.

Bewildered, speaking as much to himself as anyone else, Dolph said, "She lied about us."

"Like hell!" a ranch hand snapped at him. This was a short man built like a stump. His face reddened as he told Dolph, "Miss Vicky don't lie!"

"Stumpy," the pock-marked man said to the short one, "you got a throw rope on your saddle?"

"Uh huh." Stumpy started for his horse.

Mixed anger and fear flashed across Dolph's face. His shoulders twitched as his hands turned into fists. Tensely he shifted his weight to the balls of his feet. He looked about to lunge.

Gus lifted a hand to restrain him. "Hold on, brother. Take it easy now. This is all a mistake and we'll get it all straightened out."

"Sure," the pocked man growled sarcastically. As far as he was concerned, it was all straight now. Vicky had accused a pair of killers. For him, that settled it.

Stumpy pulled the throw rope from his saddle. He held it out to the pocked man. "Here, Des."

Gus looked at the third ranch hand. He was older than the other two. He looked less certain. Gus spoke to him. "You know lynching's against the law. They call it murder."

The third man nodded slightly. He said, "Des, he's right. It's the law's business, not ours."

"Hell," Des answered. "All the law'll do is hang them.

"Then why get yourselves into a mess of trouble doing it?" Gus said calmly. "Leave it to the law."

Now Stumpy looked doubtful. He said, "He's got a point there."

"That deputy will be here tomorrow, won't he?" Gus asked.

The third man answered, "Uh huh. Tomorrow or the next day at the latest."

"Things are a mess here now," Gus said. "He ain't gonna like it much if you've made an even worse mess of them."

Stumpy and the third man both looked like they agreed.

"Best you wait and let him straighten everything out," Gus suggested. He sounded confident that the deputy could do it easily. Far more confident than he felt. As far as he could see, the trouble here was a complete tangle. The things that had happened made no sense at all to him. He hoped the deputy was a damned clever man. He hoped by morning Vicky would come to her senses and admit the truth.

Unspeaking, Dolph looked from Gus to the ranch hands and back again. Then he glanced at the shotgun he had brought from the house.

Gus saw the dart of Dolph's eyes and he understood Dolph wanted to act. But grabbing for a gun could get Dolph killed. Gus put a hand on his brother's arm. His touch was an order for Dolph to hold on. Dolph obeyed, but Gus could sense that he didn't like it.

The three ranch hands spoke to each other with their eyes. Stumpy and the third man sided together. The first surge of Des's anger was fading. His shoulders slumped slightly as he yielded. Reluctant to admit yielding, he said, "Maybe we ought to decide after the rest of the men get back."

The other two nodded. Stumpy suggested, "We can lock them up until the deputy gets here."

Gus nodded in agreement with that himself. He didn't like the idea, but it sounded better than a lynching.

The third man asked, "Where?"

They all looked around. It was Des who suggested, "What about the root cellar? That's sound."

It was agreed. Des led the way. The other two hands followed, herding Gus and Dolph ahead of them at gunpoint.

The cellar was a cavelike room dug into the rocky slope rising behind the big house. Its door was board and batten, hung on iron hinges, with a hook-and-eye latch. Des swung the door open. Stumpy nudged Gus in the spine with the muzzle of his gun.

Gus squinted into the cellar, studying it as he asked, "You sure there's enough air in there for a man to breathe?"

"Yeah," Des grunted.

"What about water?" Gus said, stalling. He wanted to get the layout of the cellar before that door shut out the light. Gazing into the shadows, he noted the walls lined with shelves of jars of airtights. The floor was stacked with sealed kegs and stuffed gunny sacks. At least a man wouldn't starve in there.

Sounding as if it really concerned him, he insisted, "We *got* to have water!"

"We'll fetch you some," Stumpy grunted, jabbing him again.

"Look, we didn't—" Dolph started.

Gus stopped him. "Don't augur, brother. It won't do any good. This is all a mistake and we just got to wait peaceably until it gets straightened out."

"Hell," Dolph grumbled under his breath.

Gus had decided the door to the cellar was sturdy enough to keep night-roaming animals out but not strong enough to keep a determined man in. He supposed the ranch hands would put a guard on it. That could be a problem, but he figured he could solve it when the time came. He had no intention of waiting around in the cellar until the deputy came. He didn't like the idea of being locked up, and he didn't trust this trouble to straighten itself out. He figured the only safe, sure thing was to do the job himself.

But there was no point in disputing with a gun at his back. It was time now for some thinking. He could think in the darkness behind that door as easily as anywhere else. He didn't doubt that he could get out again when the time came.

Stepping into the shadows of the cellar, he said, "Come on, brother."

Reluctantly Dolph followed him in.

The door slammed shut behind them, and there was a small click as the hook was pushed through the eye.

"Dammit," Dolph said, "I don't like this at all. I don't understand it. Why would Miss Vicky want to make out that *we* shot Edward?"

Gus shrugged, then said, "She was plenty upset and she was trying hard to keep us from finding out some secret. I reckon she just went along with the idea to get herself some thinking time. Maybe, come morning, she'll set it all straight."

Standing still, he let his eyes adjust. There were enough cracks in the warped door to let in a little sunlight, but the afternoon was dying and the light scant. He could barely make out the shelves and heaped goods. Making his way to a shelf, he groped at it and found a jar. He twisted up the wire bail, slid off the glass lid, and prodded at the wax that sealed the jar. It was hard. But there was a clasp knife in his pocket. He pulled it out, opened the blade with his teeth, and pried the wax from the jar.

"What the hell are you doing?" Dolph asked.

Gus thrust two fingers into the jar. He scooped out a gooey lump of preserves. Sampling it, he told Dolph, "Plum."

"What?"

"Plum preserves." He took a mouthful, then held the jar toward his brother. "Have some. They're good."

"Hell, Gus! We're in trouble! Miss Vicky went and

let on we did a murder and them hairpins out there want
to lynch us, and we're locked up in here, and—hell!—
we're in trouble!"

"Ain't you hungry? I thought you missed nooning."
Gus took another mouthful. When he had swallowed it
down, he said, "I wonder if that Crow woman put these
up? Miss Vicky don't look much like the kind for making stuff like this."

"Dammit, don't you understand," Dolph groaned.
"Gus, they want to kill us!"

"They ain't gonna do it," Gus said. "Don't worry.
Ease off and calm down. It won't do no good going off
half cocked."

"But we shouldn't have let them lock us up like this!
We should have stood up to them!"

"And got ourselves hurt, maybe killed? Brother, they
had us outnumbered."

"Three to two? You call that outnumbered?"

"Six to two," Gus corrected. "There was three of
them and three guns."

"But—but—what the hell are we gonna do now?"

"I don't know about you, but I'm tired. Real tired.
Hungry, too. I mean to fill my belly and grab me a couple of hours sleep and do some thinking before I do
anything else." Gus took another scoop of preserves,
then licked his fingers and wiped them on his breeches.
Shoving the jar into Dolph's hand, he turned to probe
among the gunny sacks. Yams. He chose one and began
to cut away the skin.

"Then what are you gonna do?" Dolph asked impa-
tiently.

Gus shrugged and took a bite of the yam. Raw, it was
hard and stringy and didn't taste like much at all. But he
knew a man could keep going on raw yams. He swallowed some down, then told Dolph, "I reckon we're
gonna have to find out what really happened to Missus
Boswick and this feller, Rod—"

"You don't think Miss Vicky killed them?"

"Hell no. When we've found out what happened to them, then we'll find a way to prove it was Eli Tyler who killed Edward. After that we'll get the money for our ponies and get the hell home. You want a yam?"

"How could Eli have killed Edward? Eli was up to the house. He only just left good when Edward was shot."

"No, he only just left good when we heard something sounded like a shot. Edward was already dead then."

"How do you figure that?"

"Didn't you notice how stiff the body was? It ain't usual for that to happen as soon as a man dies. Takes time. Sometimes hours. Even days. I'd reckon Edward was dead at least an hour or two before we found him. I'd say Eli shot him somewhere else and hauled the body into the barn and set up everything for us to find just before he came to the house. While he had all the ranch hands out hunting me."

"Maybe so," Dolph allowed slowly. "But *somebody* had to be in the barn, or real close to it. I heard that shot. It came from the barn all right. Somebody had to be there to shoot off that gun."

"Nobody shot off any gun," Gus told him. "You recall that little fire? There was a reason for that. Eli built that fire and put a paper cartridge into it. Not right in the flames, but where the fire would burn to it in a couple of minutes. Then he hightailed it to the house and made sure he'd be right where somebody would be looking at him when the cartridge went off. Real clever, huh? Here, you sure you don't want a yam?"

Dolph frowned thoughtfully as he pondered Gus's idea. Glancing at the yam Gus shoved toward him, he grunted, "Raw?"

"A man's got to eat. Got to keep his strength up. I think we're gonna need our strength, brother. Trust me," Gus said.

Dolph made a grumbling sound in his throat. But he accepted the yam. Unspeaking, he and Gus ate the raw yams and finished off the jar of preserves. Then Gus settled himself on the ground. It was hardpacked and cold. He tried squirming his shape into it, but that didn't help much. Sitting up, he hollered toward the door. "Hey! Hey you out there! I want my bedroll!"

He got no answer. Certain there must be a guard, he added, "Hell, I'll catch the rheumatiz sleeping on this ground!"

This time there was a response. "Shut up and I'll fetch your soogans."

A shadow flickered across the dim cracks in the door.

Leaning close to Gus, Dolph whispered hopefully, "You want to take him when he brings your stuff in?"

"No. I want to sleep some. I'm tired brother. You settle down and rest. Don't fret so. Thinking will do a man more good than fretting. It'll be a lot smarter to wait until it's good and dark out there and the whole outfit is asleep before we go and do anything. Understand?" Gus said.

Dolph understood. But he felt too tight-strung to be patient. He gave in with a deep sigh.

After a few minutes the shadow flickered back across the door. It stayed, blocking the light. Gus heard the latch scrape. The door opened in.

The twilight was deep. The guard was a skylit figure in the doorway. He stood with a gun in his hand and two bedrolls at his feet.

"Stand back," he ordered.

Gus stood back, doubtful that the guard could even see him within the darkness of the cellar. It would be easy to take the man now. He felt a surge of impatience, a wanting to get this all over with. But what he had told Dolph was true. It would be smarter to rest first, and move after everyone was asleep.

He waited.

Cautiously the guard booted the bedrolls into the darkness of the cellar, then jerked the door shut and latched it again.

Gus spread his soogans and rolled himself in them. He was aware of Dolph doing the same. After a few moments he heard the pitch of Dolph's breathing change, and knew his brother was asleep. Satisfied that it was safe for him to sleep now himself, he let his eyes close.

11

There was a sound.

It intruded on Gus's dreams, jerking him suddenly awake. Lying still, listening, he could make out a murmur of voices just beyond the closed cellar door. The voices whispered, but the cracks in the door let sounds through. He could catch a few words. One voice belonged to the Crow woman. Apparently she had brought something to the guard outside.

Gus thought he could scent coffee. Likely that was what she had brought. He wished she would fetch him some, too. The cellar was cold, and his small supper hadn't been very exciting. He felt achy and hungry, and he needed to do some fancy thinking. Coffee would help.

He was tempted to holler and demand supper. But that would just wake Dolph, and then Dolph would start fretting again.

Dolph fretted too damned much. A man had to keep calm and use his head in this world, or he could tangle the trouble around him a lot worse than it was when he started. Impatience ruined green horses and got men killed.

Twisting his neck, he looked toward the cellar door. He couldn't see it at all now. The darkness was total. He figured it was full night outside. Since the Crow woman was still up, the folks in the big house might not have bedded yet. Maybe this was her last chore before she quit for the night.

In any case, it was time to do some thinking.

He lay back, relaxing, envisioning the cellar door as he had seen it before it was closed behind him. Upright planks each about the width of a man's hand. Battens across the boards near the top and bottom, and one slantways. All the boards had shown some warp and shrinkage. He was sure he could slide his knife blade between any of them. Likely he could locate the latch hook with it. Likely he could lift the hook out of the eye.

He would have to do it slow and easy so as not to attract the guard's attention. Hell, if that woman hadn't brought coffee the guard might have gone to sleep. Maybe he would anyway. The ranch hands had all done a piece of riding that day, what with hunting the lost studhorse and then hunting Gus.

With a small nod to himself, he took a deep breath. He held it and listened.

Small night sounds, mostly distant. Then a faint creak of leather. That would be the guard's gunbelt. A damp sound and a gulping, as the man outside drank his coffee. A sigh. But the guard's regular breathing was too soft for Gus to hear it. Well, maybe if the man fell asleep he'd snore.

For now, the guard was wide wake. That meant Gus might as well do some more sleeping. Turning onto his side, he let himself drift into shallow dreams.

He dreamed Vicky was coming to the cellar, bringing him hot apple pie. In his dream it was he, not Dolph, that Vicky favored, and he found himself fancying her. Only she seemed to be Dora Niles instead of Vicky, and then somehow she was both of them at once, and he was happy as hell about it.

But suddenly he was awake—sharply alert—listening to the faint snoring of the guard outside. There was another sound, a scraping that sounded like the latch hook on the door being very slowly and carefully forced from its eye.

With a shove he rolled out of the soogans and across the cellar floor. As he came up onto his knees, he groped for a shelf. His hand found a full fruit jar and hefted it. He could imagine Eli Tyler out there, creeping through the darkness to rid himself of the Widner brothers once and for all.

Crouching, with the weight of the jar in his hand, Gus was ready to lunge.

The door squeaked on its hinges as it was cautiously nudged open. And Gus was in motion.

There were plenty of stars outside, and the nightglow silhouetted the figure in the doorway. As Gus slammed toward it, he realized it was a woman.

He had expected a man holding a gun at ready to be in the doorway. He had aimed his body low, meaning to come in under the gun. He meant to knock the man down and smash the fruit jar on the gun hand, or the man's head, whichever was handiest.

It was too late to stop himself. He was ramming into the woman's legs. He knocked them out from under her. She twisted, falling across his shoulder. Dropping the fruit jar, he turned and shoved free of her.

With a sharp, startled gasp, she hit the ground.

He was afraid she'd scream. If she did that, she'd wake the ranch hands and all hell would bust loose. He threw himself down across her. She had fallen on her side. As he knelt astride her, he jerked her onto her back and clamped a hard hand over her mouth.

She made frightened animal noises in her throat as she struggled against him. One hand grasped at his face. He caught it and held it. Her other hand wrapped around his wrist, trying to force his hand away from her mouth. Her nails dug into his flesh like cat claws.

From the size, the feel, the scent of her, Gus knew it was Vicky Boswick. He had held her close against him when the ponies stampeded. And again in his dream. The feel of her body was appealing. So damned appealing. Suddenly he gave in to impulse. Jerking his hand away from her face, wrenching his wrist free of her grip, he pressed his mouth to hers.

He heard Dolph call his name. In Dolph's hand a match flared.

"Damn!" Dolph shouted.

At the sudden burst of light, Gus was breaking the kiss. He saw Dolph fling down the match. As the light went out, Dolph was charging at him. Dolph's fingers clutched at Gus's hair and jerked hard. Gus rose with the pull, coming erect on his knees.

Suddenly free of Gus's grip, Vicky squirmed away. Gus heard the rustling of her skirts and the rasp of her panicked breathing. But she didn't scream. Thank God, she didn't scream.

Dolph was pulling at Gus's head, twisting the face toward him. Gus grabbed Dolph's wrist, trying to break the hold, at the same time trying to speak, to explain somehow. But as he faced in Dolph's direction, a fist slammed into his mouth snapping his head back against the grip on his hair.

Gus had taught his kid brother to fight. He had started with the clean, fair ways of fighting. Then he had taught Dolph ugly, vicious ways to down a man, if that was what it took. Dolph had been a good pupil. As his fist swung back from Gus's face, his knee was coming up, driving toward Gus's jaw. It hit hard, grinding teeth against teeth. A sharp shock of pain raced through Gus's skull. A flash of red exploded behind his eyes.

Gus didn't want to hurt his kid brother. But, dammit, Dolph was hurting him. And for an instant Dolph had made himself vulnerable. With his knee up, his whole weight was on one leg. Gus lashed out in the darkness, hoping to hit that leg before Dolph could get the other foot planted firmly on the ground. His fist smashed into the side of Dolph's knee.

The knee buckled. As the leg went out from under him, Dolph let go Gus's hair. Gus jerked to the side, away from Dolph. Going shoulder down, he rolled. He meant to come up onto his feet, clear of Dolph and ready to hold him off until he could calm him down.

But as he rolled, he went through the doorway, and one of his outstretched hands touched soft, warm flesh. A sound of breathing was close to his ear. He realized his hand was on a man's neck. The guard was sprawled by the doorway, flat on his back. The touch hadn't disturbed him. He seemed to be in a stupor.

Discovering the guard, Gus thought of the ranch hands sleeping in the bunkhouse across the yard. It might not take as much as a scream to wake them. Sounds of scuffling could catch someone's attention. And if the ranch hands boiled out of that bunkhouse to find Vicky in the cellar, they could turn mean as hell.

Fighting Dolph here and now might be the wrong damned thing to do. Gus had to stop the fight before it got noisy. As he stopped rolling, he let himself sprawl. He lay in the starlight with his face toward the cellar, and went as limp as if he had been struck unconscious.

When his leg went out from under him, Dolph had tumbled on his back. Bouncing to his feet again, he crouched with his hands fisted, expecting Gus to charge him.

Vicky was huddled just inside the doorway. She wiped a hand across her mouth, doing it again and again, as if she were trying desperately to wipe away the taste of Gus's kiss. The motion caught Dolph's eye. He looked at her shadow figure. And then at Gus lying outside the cellar. Gus didn't look about to charge.

Dolph turned to Vicky. He kept his voice soft despite the anger burning in him. "Are you all right?"

She seemed dazed. He wanted to comfort her with his hands. But he remembered how she had shied away from his touch in the barn. His hands hovered toward her as he said, "Please, Miss Vicky, I won't hurt you. I want to help you. I'm sorry about him. I don't know what got into him."

She caught a breath. Then she moved toward Dolph. For an instant it looked like she was fainting, falling into his arms. But she pressed her face into his chest and wrapped her arms around his body. Shivering with tension, she clung to him.

Dolph's whole attention was on her. Gus took the opportunity to squirm closer to the sleeping guard. The man had to be drugged to sleep through all this, he thought. He traced a hand down the guard's body. Found the gunbelt. Found and drew the revolver from the holster.

Vicky was managing to collect herself. She pulled away from Dolph. Gus heard her say, "I was worried about you. You seemed so sick. So badly hurt."

Remembering his trickery, Dolph stammered as he told her, "I—uh—I reckon I heal quick. I'm right enough now. What happened? What are you doing out here?"

Vicky glanced toward Gus. He was still pretending unconsciousness. The hand hidden at his side now held a gun, but Vicky didn't see it. She drew herself up. Her stance, her tone, changed subtly. She spoke as if she were remembering something she had planned out beforehand, a speech she had rehearsed. "I came to help you. You've got to get away before something terrible happens to you."

"Don't you worry about us," Dolph said.

"Please. You've got to go. Now. I have horses ready for you. Please go home. Go back to Texas. Please don't ever come here again."

"I can't leave you, ma'am. Not now, with all the trouble around here," Dolph protested. "Miss Vicky, you need somebody to help you. I want to help."

"No! You've got to go!"

"But the trouble—"

"There won't be any trouble. Not if you go now."

Gus had a feeling Dolph would stand here and augur her until sunup if nothing interfered. Hell, somebody at the bunkhouse could wake up and stick a head out the door anytime. Somebody might come to relieve the guard at the cellar. Every minute Dolph and Vicky stood there talking could be bringing danger that much closer.

Gus didn't want to attract Dolph's attention away from the girl. Not quite yet. He moved slowly, hoping to get onto his feet before Dolph noticed him. Bracing himself, he started to rise.

But the motion caught Dolph's eye. Moments ago Dolph had been set for Gus to charge him. Now, suddenly, he was set again. And ready to take the fight to Gus. As Gus rose, Dolph lunged.

Gus jumped back, automatically leveling the revolver.

At the sight of the gun, Dolph instinctively froze. He was crouched like an animal ready to spring. He gazed at the gun. Then he looked up into the face of the man who held it. Into his brother's face.

There was starlight enough for Gus to see the flash of puzzlement in Dolph's eyes. Gus could understand it easily enough. In the Widner family, brothers never fought each other seriously. Not like this. But Vicky Boswick had changed that. What Dolph felt for her now was every bit as strong as his family feeling. His own behavior puzzled him. And so did Gus's behavior. The gun was an alien thing between them.

Looking down at it again, Dolph said slowly, "You won't shoot me."

"No," Gus admitted. "But I might pistol-whip the hell out of you, if you make me do it."

"No!" Vicky protested, her voice far too loud.

Gus winced at the shout. He growled at her, "Shut up, dammit! You want to waken the men?"

She jerked back as if he had slapped her. And he saw to his surprise that she really didn't want to waken the men. She was still afraid of him, but he could see that what she had come here to do was far more important to her than that fear. She wanted to get rid of the Widner brothers. She was desperate to have them leave. Now. Quietly.

She really did care for Dolph, he thought in passing. And he felt a touch of envy at the thought. But there were more important matters demanding his attention. He gestured with the gun. "If we're gonna augur all night, we'd better do it someplace else. Brother, latch that door behind you."

Dolph could see Gus's point. So could Vicky. She stepped through the doorway. Sullenly Dolph obeyed Gus's order, pulling the door shut and jabbing the hook through the eye.

Gus motioned toward the guard on the ground. "Set him up against something where he looks natural."

Dolph pulled the guard up and propped him against the door.

"Now let's us all go into the house," Gus said. He looked at Vicky. "Maybe you could fix us a pot of coffee and some vittles?"

"No! You've got to get away! You've got to go now! I have horses ready for you!"

He felt a temptation to accept the offer. Get the hell back home, away from the snarl of trouble in this valley. But he couldn't run now. Not when the family was depending on him to fetch home the money for those ponies. And not when he and his brother were under suspicion of murder.

He spoke softly, but his tone was an order, sharp and demanding. "I'd be obliged for some coffee."

Vicky shivered.

Dolph touched her arm. This time she accepted the touch as if it comforted her. He told her, "He won't hurt you. I won't let him hurt you."

Gus wanted to explain that he didn't mean her any harm. But maybe it would be a good thing if she stayed scared of him. That way maybe she would answer his questions. He made a small, significant gesture with the gun. "I'll sure as hell hurt *somebody* if any of them hairpins in the bunkhouse come poking out here and decide to make me trouble."

Vicky's shoulders slumped. Hanging her head, she said, "We'd better go inside."

Dolph took her by the hand. Very deliberately he

turned his back on Gus. Side by side, he and Vicky walked toward the house.

As Gus followed them, the gun drooped in his hand. He felt a hollowness in his gut. His brother had made a choice. Dolph had sided against him. Sided with Vicky Boswick.

Gus wondered just what the hell game she was playing.

12

Gus judged by the stars that it was around midnight. The big house ahead was dark but for a single upstairs window where soft lamplight glowed. He figured that would be Boswick's room. Someone would be sitting up with the wounded man. Likely the Crow woman.

Vicky led Dolph and Gus into the kitchen. She found a hand lamp, lit it, and held it up. By its light she looked at Dolph. Her eyes were wide and questioning, with fear deep in them. But there was concern in them, too. Gently she touched fingertips to Dolph's bruised cheek.

He put a reassuring hand on hers.

Standing in the doorway behind Dolph, Gus watched the two of them. They spoke to each other without words. He thought Dolph wanted to take Vicky into his arms. But Dolph was aware of being watched. And still angry at Gus.

There was silence. An intentional silence aimed at Gus. He could feel it, thick and heavy and uncomfortable. To break it, he said, "Coffee?"

Neither of them looked at him. Vicky seemed to purposely avoid it as she turned from Dolph. She set down the lamp and went to the range. There were coals banked in the firebox. She stirred them and tossed in kindling. As the coals spread to flames, she started for firewood. Dolph stepped in her way. With wordless understanding, he took over the job of building up the fire.

As Vicky ground beans, Dolph ladled water into the pot. They said nothing. They didn't even exchange glances. They simply worked together, two people in accord, almost as if they were doing a dance of some kind. A dance only they knew.

Gus had closed the kitchen door. He leaned his back against it. The gun was still in his hand, hanging heavily at his side, as he watched his brother with the girl. He knew there was blood on his face. Dolph's fist had smashed his lips against his teeth. He could still taste salt and he could feel the stickiness at the corners of his mouth. He wiped at it with the back of the hand that held the gun. He had never before known any Widner who had reached manhood to spill another Widner's blood in anger.

As he lifted the gun, he saw Dolph start. Dolph's eyes darted toward him. They held to his only an instant, but the look in them was icy and burning at the same time. Every small movement of that private dance was drawing Dolph closer to Vicky, further from Gus. Gus had a feeling that no matter what he might say now, Dolph wouldn't listen.

Jerking a chair away from the kitchen table, Gus seated himself. He let the hand holding the gun rest on the table. Leaning on his elbow, he waited. There were questions. So damned many questions. But it wasn't time yet to ask them. He had to wait until Dolph and Vicky had completed their dance. Until one or the other was ready to speak to him, and to listen when he spoke.

Once the coffeepot was on the stove, Vicky began to set out cups. There was nothing more for Dolph to do then, but he stayed at her side. He kept his back to his brother.

Gus felt weary as hell. It was a weariness deeper than the exhaustion of a long ride up a hard trail. It was the weariness of the years of fighting things a man couldn't see, couldn't smash down with his fist or stop cold with lead.

During the War Between the States, there had been an enemy to shoot at, but the real enemies had been the hunger and the cold and the fevers and the waiting. Always there had been the waiting for one damned thing or another. And finally there had been the helpless waiting for the end of it. The long, long waiting when every man knew that the war was lost, but the last shot hadn't yet been fired, the last words were not yet spoken, the last soldier was still to fall. Each man waited then, wondering if *he* would be the last to die.

When that war was done he had gone home only to find himself faced with a new war. A lonely war against an enemy that couldn't be seen or shot at. The war to keep his family going.

Arriving home, he had found his father ailing, bent with rheumatism, too crippled to head the family. He learned that his older brother was dead. The burden of the family and its debts had become his.

This was no war with an enemy a bullet could slay. This was a war of balancing this against that, of praying for rain during the droughts and for sun during the long storms. It was a struggle to drive cattle through lands of hostile people, into the hands of hostile buyers, across earth that was itself hostile. A struggle to pay off old bills and keep up with new ones. To keep the family fed. To keep sisters dressed decently and see them married well. To keep young brothers working in harness for the sake of the family instead of releasing them on their own hopeful hunts. A struggle to keep them all from drifting apart in despair.

Now, with Dolph's back turned coldly toward him, Gus felt as if he had lost that war. He felt tempted to speak words of surrender. Tempted to accept the horses Vicky had waiting. Ride for hell and gone and forget this whole damned valley. Ride alone toward a new land and a new life.

But there was a family back home in Texas depending on him. There were still debts, and there was still a herd of mustangs in a corral, and twenty-three hundred and fifty dollars in gold due him for the hard months of labor getting those mustangs into that corral.

"I'm not leaving without the goddamned money," he heard himself say.

He had muttered the words softly, but they seemed startlingly loud in the tense silence of the kitchen. Vicky and Dolph both turned to eye him. He looked from one to the other, feeling oddly embarrassed. Sharply he added, "And I'm damned well not leaving without the family name as clean as when I came here."

Dolph understood him, and remembered what had been forgotten during the moments of their fight. Turning to Vicky, he said, "You told them that *we* killed your brother."

She seemed to have forgotten that herself. Her eyes widened. They met his, then looked away. "I—I was so upset I didn't know what I was saying."

Gus decided it was time now to talk. He asked, "Do you know what you're saying now?"

She gave a small nod.

"Then you can tell your men different. You can explain to them. There won't be any need for Dolph and me to run."

"No!" The word squeaked out of her in a faint breath. "No, please! You have to go. You *have* to!"

"Why?" Gus insisted. "Are you afraid of the things we might find out if we stay here?"

She glanced at him, fear deep in her eyes. When she looked at Dolph again, her eyes were pleading desperately for him to agree with her.

Dolph heard the sense in what Gus said. He couldn't understand Vicky's reasons. But she had all his sympathy. He said nothing.

Harshly, cracking the words at Dolph like a whip, trying to force him to think it all through, Gus said to Vicky, "You told us you killed your ma."

She sucked breath in a small, pained gasp. Her lashes fluttered. Her eyes closed and she began to droop as if she were collapsing in a faint. Dolph grabbed her in his arms. He held her tight and glared at Gus.

Gus shook his head slowly. With a sudden jerk he jumped to his feet and wheeled toward the door. "Look out!"

Dolph flinched. So did the girl in his arms. Her eyes snapped open.

"More than one way to catch a possum," Gus said. He sank back into his chair. There was nothing at the door.

Dolph looked in question at Vicky. She was still in his arms, but now her body was taut and her eyes were wide-open. She blinked, then pulled away from him. With a whirl of her skirts, she turned her back to both of them.

Her voice was small and wild. "Damn! Oh, damn, damn, damn!"

She was starting to run for the dining room. Dolph snatched at her. He caught her wrist, spinning her to face him. His tone was hurt, and accusing. "You didn't faint! You only pretended. You—you—"

Gus supplied the word. "Lied."

"*You* lied to *me!*" Vicky snapped, speaking to Dolph. "You pretended you were injured just to get my sympathy and make a fool of me."

"Look at his face," Gus told her. "He *was* hurt. When a man gets marked like that, it hurts. He's still hurting. But he can take a lot of hurting before he starts to snivel about it."

Vicky looked at Dolph's battered face.

Gus went on, "You know who it was who marked him that way, don't you?"

She didn't answer. Dolph could see that she didn't know. Gently, fearful of hurting her, he told her, "It was Eli Tyler."

"You got any idea why Eli did it?" Gus asked her.

She had stopped fighting. She was tense, uncertain about Gus and Dolph, uncertain about herself as she listened. At least she was hearing, and thinking about what she heard. She gave a small shake of her head in reply.

"He wanted to get me and Dolph the hell away from here so we wouldn't find out what's going on," Gus said. "He's afraid we'll mess up something for him. Now you want to get us away so we won't find out something.

Have you got the same secret as Eli Tyler, Miss Vicky?"

"Eli doesn't know," she whispered, speaking to herself. "He couldn't."

"Know what?" Gus asked.

Again she shook her head. This time it was in refusal.

Gus spoke to Dolph. "She doesn't trust us. Not either of us. If she would trust us and tell us what this is all about, we might be able to help her."

"We want to help," Dolph told Vicky. "Can't you see that?"

"Nobody can help," she said weakly.

Gus went on, his tone making his guesswork sound like certain knowledge. "She's trying to protect somebody who'd be hurt if her secret got out."

She glanced at him, and he knew he had guessed right. Insistently she said, "*I* killed them. *I* hid the bodies. Edward was trying to protect me."

She might have said more but she saw Gus tense suddenly. The sound he had caught was small, but it told him something was moving behind him. He rose from his chair, turning to the dining-room door, thumbing back the hammer of the revolver.

The door burst open.

The Crow woman stood framed in the doorway. She was holding a snubbed-off Greener in her hands, and from the look on her face she was ready to use it.

The muzzle pointed directly at Gus's gut.

At the sight of it, Gus froze. He had been cocking the revolver as he swung it toward the door. But he hadn't completed the motion. In the instant of silence as he saw the woman there, the sear caught. He heard the sharp click. He knew the revolver was cocked. But it wasn't aimed. Before he could even turn it on the woman, she could trigger both barrels of that shotgun and cut him in half.

And she would, if he tried it.

Gently he eased down the hammer and set the gun on the table.

"Miss Vicky, move away," the Crow woman said.

Her meaning was clear. She wanted the girl safe from any stray shot. She meant to kill.

Vicky understood. "No!"

"They will ruin everything," the Crow woman said.

"But—but you can't just *kill* them!"

"We got to get rid of them. Nobody else saw that note. Nobody else will ever know. Everything will be the same as before."

The Crow woman knew a lot about this whole business, Gus thought. She knew enough to kill two men to keep it quiet. He stood silent, with a feeling of ice in his belly. Dammit, there was no way he could stop her from firing that gun, and no way to escape the blast.

Vicky was still standing close to Dolph. The Crow woman could gun down Gus without hurting either of them. But a shotgun blast at Dolph would take Vicky too. Vicky knew it. She kept her position, protecting Dolph.

Dolph tried telling her, "We want to help."

"The only way you can help is to leave here," she answered. "Please go. Forget about us and everything that has happened here."

"Yeah," Gus muttered, hoping that Vicky could handle the Crow woman. He wondered if the Crow woman was the one who had killed Vicky's mother and the man, Rod. He was certain Vicky hadn't done it. He didn't think she had it in her to kill.

"You'll go?" Vicky asked him.

He nodded toward the shotgun. "I reckon we ain't got much choice."

The Crow woman looked doubtful, as if she would a lot rather see them safely dead. But she accepted Vicky's will. Firmly she said to Gus, "Go."

"Brother," Gus said to Dolph, "I think we'd better get now."

Dolph didn't want to leave Vicky. But there was nothing else he could do. Not in front of that shotgun. He looked at her, his eyes asking her to change her mind.

"Please go," she said softly. She was about to start crying. Knowing it, not wanting Dolph to see her tears, she turned away from him. As she walked toward the dining room, she added, "The horses are around on the far side of the house. I packed food in the saddlebags. Be—be careful."

And then she ducked past the Crow woman, disappearing into the dining room.

"Come on," Gus said, starting for the outside door. Dolph followed reluctantly. The Crow woman walked a safe distance behind, keeping her shotgun leveled at them.

Outside, Gus darted a look at the root cellar. The guard still lay asleep on the ground. Over his shoulder Gus asked the Crow woman, "What did you give him? Will it keep him out much longer?"

"Sleeping powder," she said. "The doctor left it for Mister Boswick. He said Mister Boswick would sleep all night."

Curious, Gus asked, "Why did you do it?"

"Miss Vicky told me to."

They reached the corner of the house. As they rounded it, the Crow woman said, "You talk too much. I should kill you both. There are the horses. Go now. Quick. If you come back, I will kill you."

"Uh huh," Gus grunted as he caught up the reins of one horse. This was no mustang. It was one of Boswick's thoroughbreds. When he put a hand on the saddle, he recognized the feel of it. He held the reins out to Dolph. "Here, this is yours."

Taking the other horse, he mounted up. The saddle was his, but the boot under the fender was empty. The LeFaucheaux was gone. Dolph's rifle was probably gone from its boot, too. Vicky was sending them off unarmed.

"Go," the Crow woman insisted.

Lifting rein, Gus nudged the horse into an amble. It was a tall horse, its stride long and its gait easy. It answered the reins and his spurs with a quick willingness.

Dolph fell in at his side. They held both horses at a fast walk as they headed for the road. Neither spoke. As they reached the road, Gus glanced back.

The Crow woman was just a shadow, but he was certain she was watching them, with the shotgun still in her hand and her finger still snug against the trigger.

Dolph broke the silence. He whispered against the night, but there was a hard edge to his voice. "Brother, I don't mean to go against you, but I ain't going home yet."

"Me neither," Gus allowed.

"Huh?" Dolph had been expecting an argument.

"Brother," Gus told him, "we're set up to get killed. These ain't our horses we're on. They're wearing Boswick's brand. Come morning there's gonna be a bunch of snuffy hairpins hungry to go hunt a couple of Texicans they think killed their boss's son and stole two horses. Likely they ain't gonna be in a very pleasant mood."

"But we didn't kill—"

The blast of a shot shattered the night.

It sounded loud enough to wake the dead. It would sure as hell wake the hands in the bunkhouse.

Slamming his spurs at his mount's flanks, Gus snapped, "Damn! Come on, brother! We ain't got until morning now!"

13

It would take a little time for the ranch hands to find out what had happened, then to saddle up and ride. From the moment he heard the gunshot Gus began to gauge the time in his mind, to keep track of how far behind him pursuit might be. He figured he and Dolph had to stay out of sight of the ranch hands. The men would be mad now, ready to take action, maybe even shoot at sight. And Gus and Dolph were unarmed.

There was no moon, but the starlight was bright. The road was visible as a pair of pale traces through darker grass. The potholes were puddles of shadow. Gus and Dolph could see well enough to chance pushing their mounts. They rode hard, staying side by side in the wheel ruts. The long-legged horses were faster than the stubby mustangs they were used to, but Gus was afraid these horses wouldn't have the same kind of rawhide gut, the bottom to keep on going and going and going. He wasn't sure how long they could be pushed before they began to falter.

At least the bunch chasing them wouldn't be pushing any harder or riding any faster. If those ranch hands knew anything at all about man-chasing, they wouldn't be pushing nearly as hard or fast. They would pace their mounts and plan on catching up after Gus and Dolph had exhausted their horses.

From the feel of the animal between his legs, Gus figured that would be somewhere on the far side of town where the road twisted upslope toward the high gap. But he didn't intend to see that happen. He would have to find some better way than running until the horses gave out, then standing to be captured.

Considering possibilities, he thought of the house ahead that was stocked with guns and ammunition. If he and Dolph could reach Dora Niles's place, they could turn loose the horses and hide while the pursuing riders went on past. Then they could arm themselves from Dora's stock and backtrack to the ranch. Boswick's house was probably the last place the ranch hands would think to look for them. And it was the place to find the answers, to clear up the accusations against them.

They were covering ground fast. Gus figured Dora's house should be just beyond that point of woods up ahead. It had better be. He could feel his horse weakening. The stride was long and pounding, but not so sure or steady as it had been.

Dolph was half a length ahead of him. He called out, "Brother, you see up yonder, where the trees come almost to the road? Tie up your reins and get off quick when we get there. Send your horse packing on!"

"No!" Dolph called back. "We can't get anywhere afoot! We've got to keep ahead of them!"

"These nags can't hold the pace. We've got to go to ground—"

"Those cowboys know the woods around here and we don't. If we're afoot, they'll catch us for sure!" Dolph answered.

There was no time left to argue or explain. They were nearing the woods. Gus snapped at his brother, "You hear me!"

He was knotting his reins as he spoke. He dropped them over the saddle horn and jerked his throw rope loose from the pommel.

"You hear?" he called again.

Dolph nodded.

Gus jumped. In the same motion he was swinging the coil of rope. It slapped hard against his horse's rump.

With a startled nicker, the horse kicked out, and dashed on.

Gus hit the ground feet first. His knees bent, taking the shock, and then he was running to keep his balance. To get out of sight. Long, bounding strides took him across the narrow patch of grass between the wheel ruts and the woods. As he reached the edge of the forest, he looked back.

Dolph hadn't jumped. He was still on horseback, bent low over his mount's neck, whipping its flank with his rein ends.

Free of a rider's weight, Gus's horse had passed Dolph. Dolph seemed to be racing, determined to catch up with the loose horse. But he never would.

"Damn!" Gus grunted between his teeth.

Running, Dolph would be caught. If he were caught, he would likely be killed. Gus cursed silently to himself as he lunged into the shadows of the forest. It was too late now to stop Dolph, too late to stay with him, too late to explain and make him understand. Too late for damned near everything. But he had to do *something*. Leaning his back against a tree, dragging deep breaths, he listened and thought.

The sounds of the two horses racing away were still loud against the silence of the night. The murmur of hooves against the ground coming from the other direction was faint yet. There was some time. Not much, but maybe enough.

If it had been any man but his brother, Gus might have thought differently. A man made his own decisions, and he stood or fell by them. But this was Dolph, the young brother Gus had taught and helped grow up. If Dolph made wrong decisions, Gus felt it was his own fault for not being a better teacher. Now it was his responsibility to help Dolph, to give him another chance.

He would have to pull the ranch hands off Dolph's trail, even if it meant giving himself away. As he groped through the woods, he was thinking of that cartridge in the fire at Boswick's ranch. He could use Eli's trick. If he could make it to Dora's house and get a fistful of cartridges, he could set a decoy. Build a fire behind the house. Throw the cartridges into it and then light out for the woods. He would probably have time to hide himself before the cartridges began to explode. The sounds of "gunfire" should pull the ranch hands off Dolph's trail, over to the house. When they found Gus wasn't there, they would search. Maybe they would find him. Maybe not. It was the chance he would have to take.

He came out of the woods to one side of Dora's house. It lay dark and silent in the night. As he looked across the open field at it, he was glad he had made Dora go stay with the preacher's family. He wouldn't want to involve her in this mess.

Drawing a deep breath, he bent low and raced toward the house.

The harsh bark of a dog shattered the night stillness. It was an ugly barking that told Gus the dog meant business. And it was coming from the direction of the house. Coming toward Gus. Coming fast.

He saw the dog then, a sudden shadow streaking across the yard at him. Nearly as big as a painter-cat, and damned near as fast. The watchdog, Rex. But Rex shouldn't have been here. The dog should have been at the preacher's with Dora.

"Whoa, boy!" Gus called at the charging animal. "Easy there! It's me. You know me, boy!"

Teeth bared, Rex lunged.

Gus jumped, throwing an arm up in front of his face. The dog was quick. It was slamming into him. He struck at it with his upraised arm. His wrist caught it across the face, but its weight hit him hard. It was a big dog, and heavy. He staggered back, almost going to his knees. The dog fell away from him. Instantly it was up again, leaping at Gus as he caught his balance.

He lashed out with a fist, as if it were a man attacking him in a brawl. The fist caught the dog in the chest. The blow jolted through Gus's arm all the way to the shoulder.

The dog fell. And sprung up, charging again.

Gus was wheeling to one side, hoping to evade the dog. It threw itself at him. Glanced against him, teeth snapping. He swung his arm, slinging the dog away from him.

Even as it hit the ground, it seemed to be leaping at him again.

He couldn't outrun the damned animal. He had no way to hold his own in a fight with it. Not against those teeth. If they caught him, they would be like a bear trap locked onto him.

Jumping back, he swung his fist at the dog's head again, wondering if it were possible to knock a dog out that way. But as he jumped, his foot hit something that rolled under it. He slipped off balance. Tottered. And the dog's teeth caught his arm. He felt them sink into his flesh. Felt them grind against bone.

For a moment there was shock. A kind of numbness. A stark clarity. He knew the teeth were in his arm, but he felt no pain. Not yet.

In that moment his other hand was lashing out. The fist slammed into the side of the dog's head. It was a blow that would have staggered, maybe felled, a big man. But the dog's grip didn't break.

Then the pain was starting. It began to burn up Gus's arm, spearing through his body, wrenching like a sickness at his gut. He struck the dog's face again. And again. It didn't seem to be doing a damned bit of good. The dog was winning. The pain was driving Gus down, pressing him toward a blood-red haze. If he fell into that haze he knew he would pass out. He couldn't let himself fall. He *couldn't*—

There was a voice. Dora Niles's voice. "Rex?"

There was a light. A lamp glowing not far away. Dora was standing on the kitchen gallery, holding the lamp up, squinting into the night.

"Rex?" she called again. Then she spotted the dog. And the man. Her tone changed from question to command. "Rex! Down, Rex! Back, boy!"

The grip of teeth in Gus's arm eased. Yielded. The dog let go and began to back away. It backed just beyond Gus's reach and stood there, growling, snarling, eager to attack again.

Gus crouched with a hand wrapped over the injured arm. He felt weak as hell, and he didn't seem able to catch his breath. The red haze fogged his vision. He stood motionless, gazing at the dog through it.

"Who is it?" Dora asked warily of the dark figure crouching beyond the spill of her lamp. "Who's out there? What do you want?"

Still struggling for breath, Gus called back in hoarse gasps, "It's me. Gus Widner. Remember?"

"Of course. What is it? Has something happened to Harry?"

"No, ma'am. To me. I got to talk to you."

"Come on over here."

"The dog—"

"Come, Rex," she called. "Come sit."

The dog stood its ground a moment longer. Threat rumbled deep in its chest. Then slowly it turned. With glances over its shoulder at Gus, it ambled to the gallery.

"Come sit," Dora repeated.

The dog climbed the steps and seated itself at her side. It looked up at her, grinning, tongue lolling. There was blood smeared on its mouth. Gus's blood. But Dora didn't see that as she patted the dog's head and said firmly, "Lie down, boy."

Calm now, the dog settled itself on its belly.

"All right," Dora told Gus. "Come on ahead. He won't make any trouble."

Clutching the injured arm, eying the dog, Gus approached the gallery. Rex eyed him in turn, but didn't move.

As Gus reached the circle of lamplight, Dora asked him, "What are you doing here at this hour?"

"Getting chased by a bunch of damned fools who want to kill me," he said, thinking the ranch hands would be passing by pretty soon now. The rumble of hooves was clear and close. He asked Dora, "You hear them?"

She cocked her head and listened a moment, then nodded.

"It's all a mistake," he told her. "But they ain't gonna wait around for me to explain. I meant to hide in your house. I didn't think you'd be here. I've got to do something quick."

"Come on inside," she said, motioning with the lamp.

"I got to get them off the road and over after me," he said as he followed her inside. The dog stayed on the gallery. When Dora shut the door between it and them, Gus felt a surge of relief.

He went on to explain to Dora, "They're after my brother. He's a fool. They'll catch him for sure if I can't pull them off him and send them up a dry trail. I need a gun."

Dora set the lamp on the table and turned toward him. She saw his arm then, and the smears of blood on his shirt sleeve. "You're hurt!"

"I'll worry about that later. I've got to call them buzzards off Dolph's trail. Ma'am, I've got to have a gun. Quick!"

"You need help. Be still. I'll take care of them. Which way is your brother heading?"

"On toward town."

She nodded. Taking the lamp with her, she went through the parlor to the front door. Gus followed her. As she slipped out onto the gallery, he leaned against the wall next to the door, listening.

From the sound of the horses, the riders must be out there on the road in front of the house, near Dora's turn-off.

Dora gave a shout.

The hoofbeats slowed. Horses turned. Gus could hear them heading for the house. He heard Rex barking, racing around the house to the front. He hoped the dog would attack the riders, but he knew Dora wouldn't let that happen.

She called Rex to her side.

The horses came into the yard and stopped.

The voice that rang out was Eli Tyler's. "Dora! What's wrong?"

"Prowlers in my yard. What are you doing here, Eli?"

"We're hunting a couple of bastards who killed Edward Boswick."

"What?" Dora gasped startled. She sounded appalled.

Maybe she would believe her brother, Gus thought. He glanced around the darkness of the parlor. As far as he knew, all the guns were in the workshop. He wondered if he could find his way in there and locate a loaded gun in the darkness. He was groping for the workshop door, thinking his chance was damned slim, when he heard Dora say, "Someone ran through the yard a few minutes ago. Rex raised such a ruckus that I came out to see what was going on. I saw one man afoot. There might have been another. I thought he was a tramp. A prowler looking for something to steal. Do you suppose he—"

"Yeah!" Eli growled.

"Rex wanted to go after them," Dora said. "I was afraid they might hurt him, so I called him back."

"Which way did they go?"

"Across the back. Toward the hills behind the house."

"You heard her!" Eli shouted at the men with him. "Get the hell after them!"

"We'll never catch them in the woods in the dark," a man protested.

"Spread out," Eli ordered. "Comb the damned woods. Get them!"

Saddles creaked and bit chains jangled. Horses began to move away. Gus sighed with relief. Then he heard Eli speak again.

"Sis, I want to talk to you."

"Not now," she answered.

"This is important." His tone was confidential, as if he had a secret to share with her.

"Not now, Eli. I don't want to talk now."

"It won't take but a minute, sis."

"Not now!" she repeated emphatically. "Don't you understand me, Eli?"

"Listen, sister," he snapped at her, "you don't talk to me like that. I'm the head of this family. I always have been and I always will be!"

"No, Eli," she said. "We're partners now. Either we're partners or it's nothing at all. Understand me, Eli. I don't want to talk now. Come back later."

There was a long moment of silence. Then Eli's voice, heavy and reluctant, "All right, sis. Later."

"Be careful, Eli!" she called after him as he rode away.

She came back into the parlor. Holding up the lamp, she looked into Gus's face. "They're gone now. You'll be safe here."

She seemed sincerely concerned. And he sure as hell felt like staying. His injured arm was throbbing, the pain sucking the strength out of him. But he said, "No, I got to get going."

"Where?"

"Back to the ranch. Ma'am, there's a hell of a puzzle there, and I've got to find the answers to it, or else me and my brother may be in a mess of trouble."

"No!" she said sharply, the word cutting across his. He paused, looking at her in question.

Her tongue darted over her lips. Turning away from him, she set the lamp on a table. When she faced him again, her eyes went to his injured arm. "You're badly hurt. You can't go anywhere like this. Here, let me see it."

He let her lift the hand he'd held over the wound. Her fingers peeled the torn sleeve back from his fang-ripped flesh. Her touch was warm and gentle. Peering at the injury, she shook her head and insisted, "That *has* to be cleaned and bandaged. It could be infected. You wouldn't like gangrene to set in. You wouldn't want to lose your arm."

"No, ma'am," he allowed.

"Then you come into the kitchen and let me fix it for you right now."

It was a good feeling to have someone care. It was a good feeling to be close to a handsome woman like Dora Niles and have her speak to him in that caring way. He followed her into the kitchen. Settling himself at the table, he rested his arm and took a close look at the wound himself.

It was ugly. The dog's teeth had torn the flesh. The gashes were ragged and still oozing blood. Remembering wounds he had seen on the battlefields, and the stench of the hospital tents, he knew she was right. It had to be properly tended or it could fester and cost him the arm, maybe even his life.

Knowing that he had no choice but to stay, at least for a while, he felt some of the tension in him ease. But he couldn't really relax. Not while Dolph was still out there alone, still running.

Now that Eli and the ranch hands had been turned off his trail, Dolph might make it through the gap. He might make it to someplace that would be safe for a while. With luck, Gus thought, this whole damned mess could be settled before anyone caught up with Dolph.

With luck.

But Gus couldn't trust luck. He had to depend on himself. He would have to act soon.

He watched Dora take a bottle from a cabinet, fill a glass, then set it in front of him. He supposed it was more of the sour wine, but as he lifted the glass he caught the scent. This was whisky. Real, honest corn whisky. When he took a swallow, it bit back, rasping down his throat and burning in his belly. He emptied the glass and gave a pleased sigh. It was the first decent drinking liquor he had tasted since he left Texas.

The kitchen stove was cold. Dora kindled a fire and

added wood, then filled a kettle and set it to boil. She returned to the table, smiling slightly in a secret sort of woman way, and refilled Gus's glass for him. As he drank from it, she stood at his side, just a bit behind him. She put a warm hand on his shoulder, and he knew she was looking down at him.

"Gus," she said softly, her tone tender, "I'm afraid."

Craning his neck, he looked up at her. "Afraid?"

"For you. I don't want anything to happen to you. I want you to get home safely. You have family back in Texas, haven't you?"

He nodded.

"You have to think of them, too. You've got to go home to them. You can't take a chance on getting killed up here, so far from home."

He knew there was sense in what she said. But the family name was important, and so was the money he had come here for. And Dolph was even more important. The troubles here, and his business here, had to be settled before he could go home again.

"You've got to give it up, Gus," Dora was saying. "You've got to get away while you have the chance."

"It's important to you?" he asked.

She bent toward him, her cheek near his. Her voice was soft and husky, little more than a whisper at his ear. "Very important."

It was an invitation, and he was about to accept it. He was about to catch her mouth with his, when the kettle began to sing.

Dora made a sound of anger at the interruption. The kettle was insistent, bubbling, close to boiling over. With a sigh, Dora went to tend it. She filled a basin from it, added cool water from a bucket, and tested the temperature with her finger tips. She added a little more cool water, then brought the basin to the table.

She used clean cloths to wash the blood from Gus's arm and flush water over the gashes. Her hands were very gentle. Her voice was soft, but urgent. "You ought to see a doctor. This should be cleansed thoroughly and treated with carbolic acid."

"My ma always used brine on an open wound," he told her.

"Your mother must be worried about you, so far from home."

"She's more worried about Dolph."

Dora lifted a brow at him. "Does she care more for your brother than for you?"

"He's a lot younger and greener than I am," Gus said. "He ain't had as many years to learn how to take care of himself as I have."

"You haven't done too well taking care of yourself," she said as she finished cleaning the wound. She began to bandage it with fresh strips of cloth.

Gus considered her tone. Her whole attitude. He put obvious meaning into his voice as he said, "I reckon I really need a woman to look after me."

She darted a quick glance at his face. Sounding very serious, deeply concerned, she said, "Go home, Gus. Forget the Boswicks. Go home while you still have the chance."

"I wouldn't get far afoot. Not with that bunch hunting me like I was a loco wolf."

"I could help you. I could drive you out of the valley. You could get a horse on the other side of the gap. You could go home."

"If I was to run into that bunch on the way to the gap, I sure wouldn't want you to be with me, ma'am."

"I can put the top up on the buggy and you can hide behind the seat. If we ran into someone from the ranch, he'd know me. He wouldn't bother me. No one would doubt me. You'd be safe with me, Gus. You could go home and forget about the Boswicks."

"And about my own brother?"

She shaped a little smile that was meant to be reassuring. "He'd probably be home already when you got there."

Gus licked his lips. The taste of the whisky was on them, sweet and bitter at the same time. "You'd be taking an awful chance, ma'am."

"I don't care," she told him.

He took another sip of whisky. Then he said, "Dora, would you go with me?"

She frowned at him. "What do you mean?"

"Go home to Texas with me? Would you marry me?"

She hesitated. Looking at her own hands, she murmured, "Yes."

"Now?"

"Yes."

14

"I'll need guns," Gus said. "A handgun and a rifle. And ammunition for them both."

"I'll get them for you." Dora sounded anxious. In a hurry to get moving. Wheeling, she headed for the workshop.

Gus watched her go through the parlor door. She moved with a quick, light grace, the skirt of her robe swirling as she turned through the doorway. She was one hell of a handsome woman.

He frowned at the bandage she had been wrapping around his arm. She had forgotten to finish tying it. The ends dangled loose. He took hold of one with his good hand, caught the other with his teeth, and finished the knot.

A man had to take care of himself, he thought. He downed the rest of the whisky in the glass, sat back, and listened. The house creaked, the way houses do in the night. The cooling stove muttered to itself. Something scraped in the workshop, perhaps a sticking drawer being forced open. Outside, insects chittered. All normal sounds, all peaceful enough.

He heard more sounds from the workshop. Scratchings and scrapings. It seemed to be taking Dora a long while to find the guns and ammunition for him. At last he heard her steps coming toward the kitchen. She entered the room with her hands full.

She had brought him a holstered revolver on a buscadero belt, a lever-action rifle, and several boxes of ammunition. She dumped them all on the table. The rifle was a Winchester. The handgun looked like an army model Remington. Rising, Gus started to draw the gun from the holster, meaning to test the heft of it.

"Here, I'll help you," Dora said, pulling the gun, belt and all, from under his hand. She slung the belt around his waist for him. As she buckeld it, her head was bowed. Fine wisps of her hair tickled his chin. He thought he would kiss her when she straightened up again. But as she finished buckling the belt, she back-stepped. She moved too quickly for him to catch her mouth in an easy, natural motion. He let it go. Picking up the rifle, she told him, "We'd better hurry."

"I'll go hitch the rig while you dress," he said.

She looked at his bandaged arm. "Can you handle it?"

"Sure." He reached out for the rifle.

She put it into his hand. "I'll bring the ammunition."

He nodded and started for the back door. As he reached it, he stopped to ask, "The dog?"

She opened the door and called for Rex. The dog came in, tail wagging, tongue lolling. It gave Gus a wary glance, then looked to Dora for orders.

"Stay." She pointed to the floor beside the stove. "Stay here, Rex."

The dog sat down.

As Gus went out, Dora called after him, "Please hurry!"

"Yeah," he muttered to himself. The rifle dangled from his good hand and the revolver hung heavy against his thigh. His bandaged arm ached more than he wanted to admit. With slumped shoulders and a weary stride, he headed for the stable.

The horse was a mare, and gentle enough for a lady to handle. It didn't give him any trouble. He was grate-ful for that. He got it into harness and between the shafts, and was about to start putting the folding canvas top up on the buggy when he heard Dora coming.

She had changed into a traveling suit of some dark fabric, and wore a wide-brimmed hat with pale plumes on it. She was carrying the ammunition boxes on one arm, pressing them to her body to hold them. On the other hand she had a muff of some pale, fuzzy stuff like fur. She was wearing a scent. Gus could smell it as she came toward him. It was a faint, sweet, enticing scent full of suggestion and promise.

With a feeling of deep sadness, he turned to meet her. "Ready?"

"Yes." She sounded very excited, very tense. "Please hurry!"

He grabbed her suddenly, his fingers clamping onto the arm that held the muff. Startled, she winced. The ammunition boxes slipped out of her other arm and clattered on the ground.

"Gus!" she protested with a gasp.

He twisted her arm, increasing the biting pressure of his fingers in her flesh. She squealed with pain, and something else clattered to the ground.

Gus shoved her away. Shoved her so hard that she almost stumbled. As she staggered back, trying to catch her balance, Gus bent and snatched up the gun she had dropped. It was a small five-shot pocket pistol. She had been carrying it hidden inside the muff.

Leveling it at her Gus said, "You lie real good, lady."

"I wasn't lying. Gus, I want to help you. If you think that I—oh, no! Gus, I brought that gun so I could back you up if there was trouble."

"You brought it to use on me."

"No!"

He was shaking his head slowly, a firm denial of her words. "You lie good, but not good enough. You made a mistake coming back here from the preacher's house where I left you. You came back because you knew damned well you weren't in the danger I thought you were."

"I thought you had exaggerated," she said. "I know now that I was wrong. You were right."

Gus went on, "A while ago when your brother was at the door, you wouldn't let him talk to you because you knew I was on the other side of that door. You didn't want me to hear what he might say."

"I was afraid he'd find you and hurt you!"

"Just now, inside, you didn't want me to check out the revolver you gave me. Not there in the light. You were afraid I'd find out you'd done something to it. You've messed it up somehow so it won't do me any good."

"Gus, you're upset. You're worried and hurt and you've been drinking. You're letting your imagination make a fool of you."

"It ain't my imagination that's trying to make a fool of me. Lady, you were too willing to come along with me. Too willing to agree to marry me. This morning you were downright crazy in love with Harry Boswick. Tonight you're willing to run off with me and never see him again."

"This morning I didn't know you, Gus. I thought I loved Harry until I met you. Now it's all different." She took a tentative step toward him. Her hands were spread, pleading and inviting.

He made a small gesture with the gun. It told her to stay put. "You tell me you're willing to run off and go to Texas with me. You're willing to leave your whole life here behind you. You were gonna go away with me and never come back. But you didn't bring any luggage at all. Not one bit of clothes or one keepsake."

"I—I—I wasn't thinking about things like that. Gus, I was worrying about you. You've got to get away before they find you and kill you!"

"Lady, you figured you'd be back here right damned quick. You'd be back to tell your brother you had finished me off for him and you could go on with your plan to marry Boswick for his money. Right?"

"No! Gus, I never meant to hurt you. I wanted you to get away from Eli before he could kill you. I would have driven you through the gap. I would have left you somewhere far enough away that you'd be safe. I wanted you to go home and forget us. I couldn't go with you.

I couldn't give up everything Eli and I have worked so hard for. I couldn't leave Eli. I don't love you enough to do that, Gus. But I do care for you. I care very much. I don't want you hurt. Gus, please go home. Go now, before it's too late!"

He thought she was finally telling the truth. And it twisted in him like a knife. If things had only been a bit different, if only she hadn't been so damned ambitious, he and she might have found something together. Something very good.

He couldn't hold onto his anger. But he couldn't forgive and forget either. He still had his brother, his family, and himself to think of. With determination he said, "You go ahead and get into the buggy. We're gonna drive over to Boswick's. On the way you can tell me exactly what you and Eli have been doing. Maybe we can work this all out so that nobody else gets hurt too bad. So nobody else gets killed."

She shook her head doubtfully. Sadly, with an air of resignation, she stepped to the buggy. She gathered her skirts with one hand and grabbed the whipsocket with the other. Bracing against the whipsocket, she set a foot on the step iron. She hesitated a moment, then looked over her shoulder at Gus. Her voice was soft and small and helpless. "I need a hand up."

It was the wrong thing for her to say. It revived Gus's anger. "Lady, you live here alone and its your buggy. You've got into it plenty of times without help. You can do it again now."

"I—oh, Gus!" She sounded close to tears. Her head was partially turned and the starlight gave shape to her profile. There was a forlorn despair in the tilt of her head. Her whole air called to Gus for help.

His hands wanted to lift her into the buggy. His arms wanted to hold her close. But there were at least three people dead, and she was a party to the deaths. Gus might be dead now himself if Harry Boswick hadn't caught that bullet. And she could sure as hell lie.

He made no move to help her.

When she realized he didn't intend to help, she tightened her grip on the whipsocket and pulled herself up onto the step. She dropped her skirts as she did it. For an instant she seemed off balance, as if she might fall. She clutched at the side of the buggy and stood awkwardly on one foot. Apologetically she told him, "I must be tangled. I think my skirt is hooked on something."

She really did look as if she couldn't get herself into the buggy. The hem of her skirt was draped down over her boot. Gus thought maybe it was caught on the edge of the step iron. He bent to give it a tug.

Snatching the whip from its socket, she lashed out at him. As she moved, he jerked up and jumped back. His hand swung up the little pistol, aiming it at her as the whip popper streaked across his face.

The gun was cocked and his forefinger was tense on the trigger. At the sharp pain of the whip, he winced and almost fired the gun. But his finger didn't quite close on the trigger. For an instant he stood frozen, knowing with a stark clarity that even now he didn't want to hurt Dora Niles. Not in any way, no matter what.

That instant was enough for her. As she swung the whip, she plunged into the buggy. Sprawling on the seat, she grabbed the reins. She caught them and pulled herself up in the seat, lashing out with the whip again. This time she streaked the popper across the horse's rump.

It was a gentle, obedient little mare, unaccustomed to the whip. Stung with pain, it lunged against the harness. The buggy lurched into motion. Dora rocked back in the seat. Grabbing the dash, she rose to stand and struck out with the whip. It slashed hard across the mare's rump.

Frantically the horse threw itself into a run. At Dora's jerk of the reins, it raced toward the road. The buggy bounced wildly behind it.

Gus caught a breath that rasped in his throat and fell like a hard lump to hang in his chest. He lifted the pistol, holding it at arm's length, steadying his wrist with his other hand. His injured arm hurt like hell in that position. The pain seemed right. It belonged. This was a damned painful thing he meant to do.

He could see Dora clearly. She was standing in the buggy, a slender, wind-whipped figure in the cool starlight. Braced against the dash, she swayed as the buggy rocked and jounced.

Gus set his sights on her. But the buggy was jumping too much. He told himself that he would miss for sure. A shot would just bring those damned ranch hands out of the woods. They would come galloping back to throw a rope around his neck. What the hell good would that do him?

Slowly he lowered the gun. His arm throbbed. He rubbed at it as he stood watching Dora race away into the night.

The buggy was almost at the point where the path to the house forked from the road. It was a sharp turn. Dora was still driving hard, pushing the horse to its limit. As the mare swung into the turn, the buggy leaned out at an angle, two wheels lifting into the air. Jerked hard between the twisting shafts, the mare stumbled. The breeching slammed its rump. The buggy bucked.

Gus saw Dora's dark figure pinwheel out of the buggy. He was already running toward her as she hit the ground.

The buggy tottered, fell back onto its four wheels, and shivered. The horse was still on its feet. It began to gallop again, straight down the road, with the empty buggy rocking behind it.

Gus reached Dora's still figure and dropped to his knees. She was lying in the grass, face down, her skirts flared around her. Her arms were outflung, the hands open. Her hat was gone and her hair had come loose. It was tumbled around her head. The head was at an angle. A wrong angle. A very bad angle.

Tenderly Gus touched the hair. The soft, fine hair he had longed to run his hands through. Her face was twisted toward him. He brushed a stray lock away from her

cheek. There was blood on the cheek. A small trickle of
it had come from her ear. Just a little blood. Just a few
drops.

He. didn't have to touch her face to know. The flesh
would still be warm, but the warmth would be fading.
Already she seemed somehow smaller, as if an important substance had gone out of her, leaving only a shell
to shrink in on itself.

This was no longer Dora Niles. Dora was gone. Just a
memory now.

Even so, Gus felt an urge to shift the body into a better position—one that would have been more comfortable for a living being. His hands wanted to straighten the
skirts and close the glassy, staring eyes. He shook his
head, denying himself. He had to leave her as she had
fallen, or whoever found her there would know someone
had touched her. If Eli or one of the ranch hands found
her, it would be easy enough to guess that the one who
touched her was Gus Widner.

Rising, Gus stood and wondered why she had been
what she was instead of what she seemed to be. What
made a person willing to live a lie, willing to lie about
love, even willing to condone murder, the way Dora had
done?

The sky was changing. There were hints of false
dawn. Daylight would be coming soon. And with it, riders hunting Gus, looking to kill him. Dora was dead;
there was no changing that. Gus had to look out for
himself, and do what he could for Dolph.

With the little pocket pistol hanging from his hand, he
started for the woods.

15

The slopes of the valley were well wooded. Gus figured he should be able to make his way to the Boswick place without having to cross any open areas. But it would be tricky. The starlight washed the meadows and gave form to the edge of the forest. Within the woods the darkness was deep, almost total. To see where he was going, he had to stick close to the edge of the meadow. To keep from being seen, he had to stay within the shadows.

He had to move slowly, his hands groping ahead of him, his ears alert to every sound. He was aware of riders within the woods, blundering through the darkness. Unless he wanted to blunder around himself, he had to take each step with care, finding footing before he shifted weight from one leg to the other. He had to listen and scent for any animal that might be frightened into noisy flight by his approach.

He worked his way tediously over the small obstacles, the windfallen logs, jutting rocks, trickling streams, heavy roots, animal burrows, and potholes. He hoped he wouldn't run into any large obstacles that might force him deep into the woods, or out into the open.

The dawn light seemed to be a hell of a long time coming.

Suddenly he caught the sounds of riders. They were nearby. Compared to the creatures of the night, a horse made a hell of a racket. Its hooves crushed the fallen leaves and occasional bits of branches. At times the iron shoes struck bare rock. The saddle creaked. A loose bit chain would jangle. A bit with a cricket was as clear as a

151

whistle signaling in the darkness. And a weary, disgruntled horse talked to itself, making whimpering and huffing noises as it walked.

A rider gave off sounds, too. A holster on a belt could creak like saddle leather. Loose rowels and spur chains rattled. Even the bones of a man's joints might sometimes click. An unshaven man could make a distinguishable noise scratching his jaw. A hungry man's gut might rumble. A sigh would carry through the night. A man trying to hide himself would know better than to smoke, but one who chawed might spit, and that was a distinct sound.

There were scents as well. The strong odor of horses, the smells of saddle leather and gun oil and unwashed bodies.

Gus knew that no matter how cautiously he moved, he made small sounds and gave off scents. He had the advantage of making fewer, smaller sounds than a man moving on horseback. His scent wasn't as strong as the smell of a horse. And he was desperate. As long as a man didn't panic, desperation could hone his senses and his wits. It was a hell of an advantage.

Standing taut, as motionless as as a startled stag, he listened to the riders passing by. They weren't being cautious at all. He could hear whispered grumblings. From the tone, he knew the men were tired, frustrated by a sense of futility in searching the darkness. They rode on because they had been ordered to do it. They didn't expect to find anything.

But the night was ending. The colors of true dawn were shaping up in the eastern sky. Soon morning light would spread across the meadows and filter in among the trees. Once the sun topped the ridges, its fingers would probe through the canopy of the forest. Then hunting a man among the trees would no longer seem futile. With the coming light, Gus would be able to travel faster, but so would the hunters.

Passing him, the riders seemed to ooze by with exasperating slowness. He held tight rein on himself as he waited. At last the sounds and scent of them disappeared, and he dared move on. Silently he cursed the delay. He had a hell of a long walk to make. He wanted to get it done. Get this whole business over with.

He tripped once, and fell with a crash that sounded as loud as a powder blast to his own ears. Hitting ground, he lay motionless, listening desperately to the silence. All around him the night creatures were quiet and alert and frightened. They waited in a silence that could betray him as easily as noise might.

Finally they resumed their small chirpings and skitterings. With a soft sigh, Gus hoisted himself to his feet. The fall had jolted fresh pain into his injured arm. Cradling it in the good arm, he went on.

The night was dying. The sky beyond the meadow was pale now. Soon the sun would be showing itself above the eastern ridges.

As the night-prowling creatures returned to their burrows and dens, the day creatures rose to meet the dawn. The sounds of the forest changed. Birds began to call. A mocker screeched and swooped at Gus, threatening attack, as he came too close to its nesting place. He ducked to the side, trying to avoid the bird. A mocker would attack a man, and make one hell of a racket doing it, if it thought the man meant danger to its nestlings. The last thing he needed now was a bird mad at him. Evading it, he kept going.

He was tired. Too damned tired. His legs ached, and his arm throbbed, and his thoughts wanted to drift. He had a feeling he was in the war again, separated from his outfit, trying to pass through enemy lines, and for an instant he couldn't figure out what had happened to his gun. He realized dreams were trying to force themselves into his mind. With a shake of his head, he pulled himself back to the here and now. Too damned tired.

The sun was a raging flame on the far ridge when he suddenly became aware of horses. He froze, gently scenting the air. Horses and men. He heart a faint rustling, a squeal of leather on leather, and almost winced at the nearness of the sounds. The men were right ahead of him, just beyond a small thicket. Apparently they had stopped to rest a while. And he had almost blundered into them.

As he paused, he heard another noise—that certain sigh of leather a saddle makes as a man mounts up. Then the horses began to move. They were coming toward him, around the thicket. He glanced around desperately. He knew the feeling of a trapped animal. But he wasn't caught yet. Dropping to his belly, he slithered toward a windfall,

The log was big and old, with some tangles of underbrush growing around it. One end of it lay on an outcrop of rock, held a few inches above the ground. There was a hollow under it. Not enough of a hole for him to slip into, but maybe enough to help. He squeezed close against the log, forcing himself as far into the hollow as he could. He lay with his face turned to the log. His eyes were closed. A man's face could betray him. Open, the eyes could catch glints of light. Closed, the lids might twitch. A jaw muscle might jerk. Any motion, no matter how small, could catch attention.

The forest animals knew the advantages of stillness. A fawn, its colors those of the woods, could huddle as motionless as a rock, making itself invisible to a casual glance. Even a searching eye could miss one hidden in thin brush.

Gus's clothes were dunned with age and travel. He wore no bright bits of color or shiny metal that might draw attention. Within the woods the dawnlight was still dull. Like the fawn, he blended himself with his surroundings. He lay in a shadow, breath held, as still as the log he was pressed against.

Small sounds spoke to him. The fall of hooves told him how close the riders were. He could hear the men and animals drawing breath. One rider spat. There was weariness and disgust in the sound.

Gus felt a deep weariness and disgust himself. Disgust at his own weariness. He had let exhaustion dull his sen-

ses. He had almost walked into the searchers. Almost
betrayed himself.

Now he lay with the breath locked in his chest and
the blood pounding in his veins. He could feel his lungs
knot with the need for fresh air. He didn't dare breathe.
The riders were still too close. A small pain was starting
in his head. His back itched. A muscle in his face quivered and there was nothing he could do to stop it.

He waited.

One of the riders spoke. He didn't bother to whisper.
"Maybe some of the others got them by now."

"There would have been hollering and shooting if
they did," another answered. "Hell, there can't nobody
find a man afoot in the woods in the dark. What we
need is dogs to track with."

"It's coming light now. Likely they'll get took pretty
soon."

"I damn sure hope so. I'm hungry."

"I hope them others catch 'em and kill the bastards.
You got a chaw on you?"

Gus heard a saddle creak as weight shifted in it. He
was aware of a man patting a pocket. He could make
out the sounds of teeth cutting into a plug.

"Obliged." The word was spoken through a full cud.

The other man grunted in response, then said, "I ever
tell you about that cat-hound I had down in Sonora?"

The horses plodded on. The sounds faded.

Gus let out the held breath in a painful sigh. He
gulped fresh air, and the shock of it set his head spinning. He lay still, breathing slowly, easing the cramp in
his chest, letting his head settle, then simply resting because it was so much easier than moving.

Suddenly he realized he had dozed. Angry at himself,
he scrambled up, checked the pocket pistol, and began
to walk determinedly on.

He considered possibilities. Dolph could be safe now.
There hadn't been any shouting or shooting. If Dolph
had been taken, there would have been excitement, and
the sound of shots would have carried a long way in this

valley, especially at night. So maybe Eli had all of the ranch hands here in the woods, hunting Gus, and Dolph was on his way through the gap unhindered.

Or maybe Eli had split up his men, sending some into the woods and the rest on up the road. Maybe Dolph had been taken beyond earshot. Maybe he was limp over his saddle, or swaying under a tree limb now.

Maybe not.

Not knowing was worse than a toothache. It was a steady distraction at the back of his mind, gnawing away at his thoughts. He shook his head and concentrated on the ranch, on what had to be done there.

The rising sun brought up a breeze. It came along the length of the valley, carrying the scents of the ranch: barn smells, odors of horses and cattle, hogs and chickens, and a faint tang of wood smoke and coffee cooking.

Gus wished to hell he had a cup of coffee. He felt so damned tired. Too tired to keep going. His gut ached and his feet hurt and suddenly he couldn't take another step. He slumped where he was. Sitting on the ground with his back against a tree, he stretched his legs out in front of him. Muscles in them jumped.

Back home in Texas, a man never walked far. Not when he had a horse. Gus hadn't done much long walking since the war. He felt as if he were in the war again, in a long, hungry retreat, desperate for an end to it all. Desperate for an end to the fighting, the killing, the dying. There had been too much dying.

Poor Dora.

Thoughts of violent death were ugly. Painful. But Gus couldn't deny them. He couldn't just turn his back and forget it all. Not with the image of Dora's twisted neck vivid in his mind. Not with the awareness that Dolph's neck would be just as twisted by a lynch rope. Not with the knowing that Eli Tyler had a rope ready for his own neck.

There were times when a man had no choice. He kept going, and did what had to be done.

Rising, Gus went on.

The sun had moved up off the ridges and burned away the dew dampness. The long shadows were sharp, the day turning bright, when he sighted the ranch. Standing at the edge of the wood, leaning against a slim shivering aspen, he looked across the meadow and the hardpack of the yard at the big stone house.

There was a saddled horse in front of the house. Just one horse, and it didn't look like one of Boswick's fancy thoroughbreds.

Smoke curled from the kitchen chimney, but the stove-pipe at the cookshack looked cold. Nobody was in there fixing a square meal for the ranch hands who had gone out during the night. Likely the coosie was with the searchers. Maybe there were no ranch hands at all left on the place now.

Who did that saddle horse belong to, he wondered.

He scanned the edge of the woods as it curved back around the ranch buildings. He couldn't simply walk across the yard. That Crow woman could use a gun, and she would, if she thought she had reason enough. He didn't want her spotting him. He would have to stay under cover until he got as close to the house as possible.

Whoever belonged to that horse should come out and ride away, or else tend the animal.

Gus waited.

The Crow woman came from the kitchen, carrying a pan. Clucking, she tossed its contents on the ground behind the house. Chickens raced across the yard to grab up whatever scraps she had thrown to them.

He thought of the shotgun she had pointed at him last night, and the shot that had alerted the ranch hands to go chasing after him. He watched the woman as if he were sighting her over a gun barrel. She was an easy target as she turned her back to go into the kitchen again. If she hadn't interrupted last night, and driven him and Dolph off to be hunted down, he might have gotten at the truth then. Dora Niles would still be alive. Dolph would be safe.

He frowned at himself. A few days ago he would

have been appalled at the idea of bushwhacking a woman. Weariness, worry, despair changed a man's mind about what he was willing to do. He had learned that during the war.

At first they had all been decent men, the Rebs and Yanks alike. Men with a sense of honor. You only shot at the enemy when he was in a position to shoot at you. You gave him a fair chance, and he gave you one. But by the end, by the time they were all half-starved, half-dead with exhaustion and exposure, a man shot at the enemy any damned chance he got.

He thought he could have killed the Crow woman now, if he'd had a rifle. But she was beyond range of the little pocket pistol he held. So he watched her go back into the house, and hated her, and felt a disgust at himself for his own thoughts. Once a man lost his sense of honor, his self-respect, he was nothing.

He shook off his drifting thoughts as he saw someone come out onto the front gallery of the big house. It was the doctor, his black bag in one hand and his hat in the other. Pausing, he exchanged a few words with someone inside the doorway. Then he put on his hat and went down to the saddle horse. Mounting, he rode away.

Gus waited until he was out of sight.

Now it was time.

16

The pocket pistol Gus carried was small. Its range was short. But within that range it could be as deadly as any other gun. He checked it again.

His mouth was dry. He licked at his cracking lips. His legs ached as he began to walk. He flexed the fingers of his injured arm, feeling small shocks of pain in the muscles as they moved. The arm was stiff and sore, but the hand worked. He would have the use of it when he needed it. He was thankful for that.

He skirted the woods, moving toward the little knoll behind the house, thinking of the shadowed figure he had glimpsed there after the sudden shot that downed Boswick. He reached the knoll and paused among the trees where they came closest to the house.

The chickens that the Crow woman had fed were still grubbing around near the kitchen stoop. He would have to approach slowly if he didn't want to chance startling them into squawking. Carrying the gun cocked, holding it down at his side, he walked toward the house. The chickens eyed him suspiciously. They edged away as he neared them. But they made no warning noises. He climbed the stairs and stopped at the kitchen door to listen.

Someone was moving around inside. He heard a clatter of dishes. Some splashing of water. No voices. He thought there was just one person in the kitchen. Probably the Crow woman.

With his left hand he gently turned the knob. He had

the gun up, leveled and ready, as he yanked the door
open.

The Crow woman was standing at the dry sink with a
soapy dishrag in one hand and a dinner plate in the other. She wheeled toward the door as it opened. At the
sight of Gus, she screeched and sent the plate skimming
toward his head.

He jumped, ducking. The edge of the plate touched
his hair as it spun past. It shattered on the wall beside
him. And he saw the Crow woman grope into the dish-
pan. He knew she was hunting another weapon in the
water. His forefinger tightened on the trigger of the pistol. But not enough to release the sear. He couldn't
shoot her. Not like this. Easing the hammer down with
his thumb, he lunged at her. He meant to use the little
gun to buffalo her.

Her hand came out of the water holding a butcher
knife. A big, ugly blade. She swung it up, the point driving toward his chest as he hit her.

His hand slammed into her face, along the jaw under
the ear. The pocket pistol was light, but its weight added
to the blow. A shock of pain shot up Gus's arm as his
knuckles rammed into bone. He felt the butcher knife
snag his shirt. It's point skidded along his ribs. The
Crow woman staggered back against the dry sink. The
knife slipped out of her hand. As she crumpled, Gus
kicked quickly at the knife, sending it spinning away before she could snatch it up again. But she made no move
to grab at it. She sprawled limply on the floor.

Dropping to one knee, he felt her face. The muzzle of
the pistol had torn her cheek. There was a little blood.
He touched a fingertip to it, then laid his palm against
her throat. He could feel a healthy throbbing there. Her
breathing seemed normal. Her jaw didn't feel broken.
He thought he hadn't hurt her seriously, and was relieved. He didn't want to hurt anyone.

He began to rip pieces from her petticoat to tie her
with. As he did so, he was aware of sounds from within
the house. Someone was walking around upstairs. He

heard hurrying footsteps. Delicate steps that had to be Vicky Boswick's. They reached the staircase and started down.

Quickly Gus lashed the Crow woman's hands together. He bound her ankles, then jammed a wad of cloth into her mouth and tied it there.

From another room Vicky called, "Maria? Maria, I heard noises. Is everything all right?"

She was coming into the kitchen. Gus swung to his feet and flattened himself against the wall, next to the open door into the dining room.

Vicky came through the doorway. She saw the Crow woman on the floor and stopped short with a small gasp. She was just a step inside the kitchen. Just far enough. Gus was beside her, a little behind her. He threw an arm around her neck. His hand went for her face. It clamped over her mouth, catching the scream that had begun in her throat. The pistol was in his other hand. He jabbed it into her back.

"This is a gun. I *could* kill you." His voice was hoarse and harsh. It sounded vicious. He hadn't meant it to sound that way. He only wanted to warn her that he had control, that she had to obey him.

Despite her fear, there was courage in her. She struggled against him. Under his hand, her mouth was open. Her teeth found the flesh of his palm and sunk in.

She bit hard. Jerking his hand away, he snapped, "Stop that, dammit! I don't want to hurt you!"

As the hand released her, she twisted away from him. She leaped back and sucked the breath to scream.

"Screaming won't help," he told her. "There's nobody around to hear you, except maybe your pa. You want to scare hell out of him?"

The scream died in her throat. For a piece of an instant her eyes were on Gus, wide and fearful, burning with despair. Then she was wheeling, dashing out of the room, slamming the dining-room door behind her.

He raced after her.

She reached the parlor and snatched a shotgun from a rack.

He dropped the pistol and lunged at her with both hands outstretched. As she swung the shotgun toward him, his fingers locked around the barrel. He shoved hard, twisting the muzzle away from his body. She had managed to get the gun cocked. As he wrenched at it, it went off. He felt the kick in his wrists, the searing sting in his palms. The blast flashed close to his face, its brilliance blinding him for a moment. A billow of bitter smoke burned in his nostrils.

But the shot all went clear. It slammed into the wall, tearing through, leaving a sudden jagged hole in the wood.

His eyes hazed and watering, his throat rasped with coughing, Gus clung to the gun. Bracing himself, he jerked it away from the girl.

She had her forefinger through the trigger guard. The guard caught and pinched it before she could pull it free. Backstepping, she raised the finger to her mouth. Like a child, she sucked the hurt.

There was wildness in her eyes as she stared at Gus. A horrified, frantic wildness. Slowly, with a jerky movement, she took the hand away from her face. And then she began to curse.

Her voice was soft and lilting, a lovely, well-trained voice that could make music of any words. But she could only have learned these words behind the bunkhouse when the men didn't know she was around.

Suddenly Gus began to laugh.

He didn't really think it was funny. Not at all. But he had been strung so damned tight inside for so damned long, and suddenly her cursing snapped the tension in him. It shattered into laughter.

She stopped cursing. As she stared at him, tears formed on her lashes. She looked like a little girl whose feelings had been hurt by adult callousness. Her fine pink mouth pouted. Her moist, angry eyes reproached him.

Suddenly she darted to the sofa. Grabbing up a pillow, she flung it at him.

He caught it easily with one hand.

She threw a specimen rock from the collection on the tabouret.

He ducked the rock, and ducked again as she sent a stuffed squirrel skimming at his head. Holding the shotgun with one hand, he gripped the pillow in the other and used it as a shield to fend off the harder objects she was hurling at him.

He understood her fighting desperation and admired her for it, even if she didn't know how to make good use of it. He didn't try to stop her, but just defended himself, waiting for her to weary of the useless battle.

Finally she paused. She had an old quilled Sioux tobacco pouch lifted to throw. It was a little thing, a soft thing that could hardly harm him. She looked from him to the pouch and saw the futility of it. Her shoulders slumped. She set the pouch down gently. Then, with a sigh of utter exhaustion, she sank onto the sofa.

She looked very small, very young and lovely, sitting there with her head bowed. Her hair, wrapped in a bun at the back of her head, was coming loose. As he looked at her, Gus felt an urge to tuck in the stray locks. He wanted to comfort her.

In a thin little voice, she asked him, "Are you going to kill us?"

That hurt. He remembered how close he had come to backshooting the Crow woman out there in the yard. How close he had come to being no better than Vicky Boswick thought he was.

He heard himself say, "I'm tired."

She looked up at him from under her brows. Her eyes were puzzled. Searching. Suddenly she said, "Where's your brother?"

"Maybe dead."

"What!"

"That mob you sent after him and me was in a lynch mood."

"No!"

"Lady, what did you expect? You told them Dolph and me killed your brother. Likely they figure now that I shot your pa, too. They're hunting me right this minute. Dolph and me got split up. I don't know if they're still after him or not. Maybe they caught him. Maybe they've already killed him. You understand? You understand that if he's dead, *you* killed him?"

"No!" she protested. "No, no, no, no!"

"You sent that mob after us," he said coldly.

"I didn't!"

"That Crow woman did, and she did it for you. You sent us running without guns to defend ourselves, and she fired the shot that sent your crew after us."

"It wasn't Maria!" she shook her head violently in denial. "It was Eli who fired that shot. I meant for you to get away. To go home. To leave us alone. But Eli saw you leaving. He turned out the men. I couldn't stop them!"

He thought she was telling the truth, and he felt a deep relief that she hadn't sent the men. But it was only a momentary relief.

"Don't let them hurt him!" she was saying. Her hands were clasped, and he wasn't sure whether she was speaking to him or praying.

He told her, "You're the only one who can stop it."

"How?"

"Get your men back in here. Tell them the truth. Do it fast."

She glanced around as if she were hunting a way to do it. Again she asked, "How?"

"You've got some way of calling them in, ain't you? A bell or something?"

"Yes! Yes, the bell!" She came to her feet quickly. Gathering her skirts, she hurried toward the door.

Gus followed her across the yard to the cookshack. The bell was the kind a locomotive carried, mounted in a yoke on a pole. Holding the shotgun in one hand, he jerked the rope with the other.

The clanging of the bell echoed wildly off the slope behind the ranch buildings. It was loud enough to call the spirits down from the high places. Gus hoped it was loud enough to reach the men who were hunting him. And the men who might still be hunting Dolph.

He let go the rope. It took several moments for the last echoes to bound down the valley and die. The silence that followed seemed hollow and drawn thin, as if the whole valley were taut with waiting. Scanning the land for some sign of the riders returning, he asked, "When they get here, what are you going to say to them?"

She hesitated. When she spoke, her voice was very small, as if it hoped to hide from him. "That *I* did it."

"That's not the truth," he said.

"I'll give them Edward's note. Then they won't blame you and Dolph for anything."

"But that note isn't the truth either."

She eyed him in question.

"You knew that your ma and her friend were dead," he said. "You knew it before we found that note."

Reluctantly she nodded.

"You knew Edward didn't kill them."

"*I* did it," she insisted.

"No, ma'am. You didn't kill Edward, and the way I see it, he was murdered by the same one who killed your ma and—"

"He couldn't have!" she gasped.

As if he knew who she meant, Gus said, "Why not?"

"He's too ill! He's barely conscious!"

"You mean your pa?"

She realized then what she had told him. Fear flashed in her eyes. A stark fear full of sorrow. Her chin quivered. Her lips moved, and Gus thought she was about to deny it, to lie again.

But it was too late now for more lies. She understood that. Slowly she nodded. It was a small nod, almost imperceptible, but it was the truth.

At the sight of it, Gus felt some of his own tension

ease. He was certain that from now on it would all be the truth. She wouldn't try to lie to him again.

Gently he said, "You wanted to protect him, didn't you?"

She gave another little nod and tried to meet his eyes. She couldn't quite manage it. Head bowed, she murmured, "It's all so terrible. I . . . I . . ."

Her voice faded. Suddenly she was folding up.

Dropping the shotgun, Gus caught her in his arms. She leaned limp on his chest. Her forehead pressed damply against his cheek.

"Miss Vicky?" he said.

There was no response. Her faint was real, and deep. Her flesh felt very cold. He had to do something for her.

His injured arm ached as he scooped her up and carried her toward the house. He hardly noticed it. He hardly noticed anything except the slackness of her body and the frightening pallor of her face.

17

The kitchen door was ajar. Gus kicked it open. And found himself facing the Crow woman.

The strips of cloth he had tied her with were scattered on the floor. She had struggled her way free of them. She was just pulling the gag out of her mouth, at the same time clambering to her feet, as Gus came through the door. At the sight of him, she dove for the butcher knife lying on the floor. It was halfway across the room. Hitting the floor, she snatched up the knife, rolled, and came to her feet. She was quick as a cat. As she scrambled up, the knife was raised, a gleaming threat in her hand.

Vicky's limp body filled Gus's arms. He stood in the doorway, holding the girl. "Dammit!" he snapped at the Crow woman. "Can't you see Miss Vicky's fainted. Help me with her."

"If you've hurt her, I'll kill you!" the Crow woman screeched, still poised to drive the knife blade at him.

"I ain't hurt her. I don't mean to hurt her. You want to help me with her or not?" He pushed past the Crow woman, carrying Vicky toward the parlor.

Knife in hand, the Crow woman followed him. He could feel her eyes on his back. He could imagine the feel of that blade plunging in between his ribs. He hoped to hell that his judgment was sound, that the Crow woman wouldn't make a move against him as long as he had Vicky in his arms.

Vicky stirred. She sighed and her eyelids fluttered. The lashes lifted slightly. The pupils under them were unfocused. She squinted at Gus's face and said thinly, "Dolph?"

"Put her down," the Crow woman told Gus.

He wasn't obeying the order. He was doing what needed to be done as he lowered Vicky to the sofa. Gently he slid his arms from under her. And spun. He slammed the side of an open hand at the Crow woman's wrist. It struck hard, sending the knife flying out of her grip.

She flung herself at him, as if she thought she could down him barehanded.

He swung at her again, his hand fisted, aiming for her jaw. Swung as if she were a man.

She saw it coming and jerked back. The blow glanced off the side of her head. Not hard enough to down her but enough to rock her. She staggered, almost tripping. As she caught her balance, she crouched to attack.

"Maria!" Vicky gasped, dragging herself up to sit on the sofa. "Stop that!"

The Crow woman paused, glancing at Vicky, confusion in her eyes.

"It's all over," Vicky said.

The Crow woman shook her head. She wasn't ready to give up. She was willing to face Gus, to fight him as if she were a man.

They were a hell of a pair, these two, Gus thought. Both of them were fighters. The Crow woman was strong and tough. Vicky had sand. She had come close to snapping more than once, but she had managed to regain control of herself. A little more time, a little more experience with life, and likely she would learn to handle herself.

Again Vicky said, "It's all over."

The Crow woman yielded reluctantly. With the look of a snarling animal, she eyed Gus.

"Can you ride a horse?" he asked her.

She nodded warily.

"Then you go saddle one and ride. You find the ranch hands. They must all be off beyond the sound of that bell or something. Way out in the woods past Dora Niles's place. You tell them to forget about hunting me and my brother and to get the hell back here to the ranch. You tell them it's Miss Vicky's order. Whatever Eli Tyler says, you stop the men from hunting Dolph, you hear?"

The Crow woman heard. But she looked to Vicky for her orders.

"Please hurry!" Vicky told her.

With a nod the Crow woman left.

Vicky turned to Gus then. Her face was still very pale. There was a tremor in her voice. "Can we stop them in time?"

"I don't know," Gus said wearily. He hoped to hell they could. He hoped this was the end of it. His injured arm was throbbing, and he could feel the dampness of blood soaking through the bandage Dora Niles had put on it.

Vicky saw the blood. "You're hurt!"

He nodded.

"Is there anyting I can do?" she asked.

"Yeah." He let go the arm and tugged the bandana from his neck. He held it out to her. "Tie this tight over it. Maybe it'll stop the bleeding."

She reached for the bandana. Her fingers touched it, then drew back. "That's filthy."

"It's what I got."

The color was coming back to her face, and the strength to her voice. "Let me see your arm."

He held it out to her.

"What happened?" she asked.

"A dog bit me."

The bandage had slipped and was working loose. She told him, "That needs a fresh bandage. Come into the kitchen and I'll fix it for you."

She started to her feet. Suddenly she swayed dizzily. He grabbed her shoulder to steady her. "You all right?"

"Yes," she said, but she didn't sound all right. She sounded as if she might faint again.

"You wait a minute," Gus told her. He went into Boswick's office and found the bottle of weak whisky that Boswick had fed to him and Dolph. Uncapping it, he took a long drink. He wiped the mouth of the bottle and carried it back to the parlor. Holding it out to Vicky, he said, "Here, take a swallow of this."

She looked disconcerted. "I don't drink."

He realized she didn't consider it proper for a lady to take strong spirits. If circumstances had been different, she might have been insulted by his suggestion. But she had more important matters on her mind now.

There were times when a person had to forget about the things folks called proper and do what made sense. Her face was still pale and her hands were trembling slightly. She needed something to stir her blood. He said, "Go on, take a drink of this. It'll make you feel better."

"Will it?" She looked up at him. There was irony in her voice and deep sadness in her eyes. "Poor Papa. Poor Dolph. Poor Edward. Will anything really help?"

"The truth might," he suggested.

She considered that, then accepted the bottle from him. The small sip she took caught in her throat. She coughed and gasped. When she caught her breath, she asked, "Do you drink much of that?"

"Sometimes," he allowed as he stepped to the window. He looked out across the yard toward the woods. There was still no sign of riders. He was afraid they had given up searching the forest and had gone back to the road, back to the trail of the horses. Maybe they had already caught up with Dolph. Maybe it was too late . . .

"Does Dolph?" Vicky was asking.

Gus turned from his thoughts to look at her. "Does he what?"

"Drink much of this?"

"Sometimes."

Cautiously she tried another sip of the whisky. This time she managed not to choke. She smiled slightly at herself, then nodded at Gus's arm. "Come on into the kitchen and I'll do something about that bandage for you."

"You kind of like Dolph?" he asked as he followed her.

Her back was to him. She gave a shy little nod.

"You don't know much about him," he said. "You hardly even met him."

"It doesn't take long," she murmured. Keeping her back to him, she busied herself with filling a basin and hunting up a handful of clean rags.

She was right about that, he thought as he seated himself at the table. Just a few hours ago he had been sitting at Dora Niles's table the same way, with his injured arm stretched out in front of him, and Dora had been fetching bandaging for it. He had hardly known Dora. Hell, he hadn't known her at all. He had only spent a few minutes with her, only exchanged a few words. But his feeling for her had been strong. So strong that the memory of her was more painful than the wound in his arm.

He tried telling himself that it was only the hunger a man on the trail always got for a woman's company. He suggested to himself that he would have felt the same way about any fairly handsome woman he met at the time, and that the feeling would pass as soon as he met another woman. But he didn't believe it.

He watched Vicky, admiring her, wanting her, and aware of the difference in his want. This was the trail hunger, the simple want of a pretty woman. He wondered about Dolph's feeling for her. And about her feeling for Dolph. Was it real or just a passing fancy? Would either of them ever get the chance to find out?

The color was all back in Vicky's face when she came to pull the dirty bandage off his arm. Her hands were steady. She had control of herself. He thought maybe she would be able to talk to him now.

As she washed the wound, he asked her, "Miss Vicky, what gave you the notion your pa killed your ma and her friend?"

She flinched, her fingers clamping on his arm, sending a shock of pain through it.

Holding himself taut against the pain, holding his voice level and gentle, he said, "You've got to tell me about it."

She pulled her hand away from his arm. She had gotten blood on her fingers. She looked at the blood. With a jerk she grabbed the damp cloth and wiped it away. Rising, turning to put her back to Gus, she said, "Would you like some coffee?"

She wasn't ready yet. He would have to wait. Or else force her to talk. He didn't want to hurt her. There was still no sound of riders approaching the house. He supposed he could wait. He said, "I'd be obliged."

The stove was cold. She got the fire started and put the pot on to heat. At last she faced him again. She looked toward him, but not exactly at him. Her eyes seemed to gaze through him into her own thoughts. Stiffly, struggling to do it, she said, "Papa wanted a divorce. Mama wouldn't give it to him."

"He wanted to marry Dora Niles," he said, meaning to help her.

"Yes. How did you know about Dora?"

"I met her." There was a sadness in his voice. He hoped Vicky wouldn't notice it. Softly he added, "She's dead now."

"Oh no! Poor Papa!" Vicky's eyes widened suddenly, as a sharp thought startled her. "Was she—was she *murdered?*"

"She fell out of her buggy. Broke her neck," he said. He didn't think there was any point in telling Vicky how it had come about. No reason to slur a dead woman's name. Not Dora's name. Not if he could help it.

Vicky looked as if she were about to ask something. Maybe something he wouldn't want to answer. He interrupted before she could speak. "You tell me about your ma and pa."

She took a deep breath. It wasn't easy for her to talk about it. Collecting herself, she began, "They weren't very happy together. They might have been once, a long time ago, but as far back as I can remember, they weren't happy. Mama was always nagging Papa to go back to England. He wouldn't go. He loves it here too much. Mama should have given him the divorce, but she wouldn't. When he asked for it, she got very nasty. She was a proud woman, from a fine old family with a fine name. Not much else, but a fine name."

He could hear the bitterness in her voice, as if she hadn't had much love for her mother. Or as if her love had been twisted all out of shape into something ugly.

Turning, she looked at the coffeepot, hoping it would offer her a distraction. But it was a big pot, and the stove had been cold. It sat silent.

With her back to Gus, she said, "Mama betrayed us all."

"Ma'am?"

She faced him again. "Rod—that's Rod Stamford— he was the son of an old school chum of Papa's. He came to visit us. He was a very nice young man. Much younger than Mama. We never imagined—I didn't—he seemed as if he were interested in me. I thought he was courting me."

Gus understood that she had enjoyed Rod's attentions. Maybe she had even considered them seriously.

She went on, "They were very discreet, Mama and Rod. No one had any idea—then I found the note."

"What note?"

"It was in the typewriting machine. I don't know who put it there. Papa has shown half the people in the valley how the pterotype works. Just about everyone on the ranch who can write can operate it. It's not hard at all."

"What did the note say?" he asked.

"That Mama and Rod—that they were going to be meeting in the woods that night. It was meant for Papa. I know it was. I thought I had found it before he saw it. I didn't want him to see it. I burned it. I didn't think he knew about it at all—until I found them both dead."

"What?"

"I followed them." The admission embarrassed her. It brought color to her cheeks. She didn't quite meet Gus's eyes. "I didn't intend to. I never wanted to. I meant to forget it, but I couldn't. That night in my room, I couldn't sleep. I just kept thinking and thinking and hoping it was all a lie. Finally, I *had* to know. I dressed and sneaked out. I was almost there, almost at the place the note mentioned, when I heard shots. Two shots. I rushed to—I found them both. Papa had gotten there before me. He had killed them both."

She stopped talking. Her eyes glazed as she stared past Gus at that dark memory.

He was sorry to force her back to such a painful memory, but he had to know the truth. All of the truth. He waited, hoping she would go on. When she didn't, he asked, "What happened then?"

It took a long, thoughtful moment before she spoke. "I was terribly afraid for Papa. Afraid he'd be caught and hanged. I couldn't let that happen. I called to him, but he didn't answer. I couldn't find him. So I went back to the house and got Maria. She helped me. We hid the bodies."

He didn't think the Crow woman would have betrayed Vicky. He asked, "Did you tell anybody else?"

"No. Just Maria. She's very dear. She's been as much of a mother to me as Mama ever was. I know we did wrong, but we had to protect Papa."

"It wasn't your pa who did it," he told her.

She frowned at him. Hoping he would convince her she was mistaken, she said slowly, "It *had* to be Papa."

"Ma'am, there ain't a jury in this part of the country that would convict a man for killing a wife he catches cheating on him. Your pa wasn't afraid of any scandal. Not if he was willing to let Missus Boswick divorce him. If he had killed her like you thought, he would have said so and got it over with so he'd be free to marry Dora Niles."

"I—I—" she stammered. She gave a shake of her

head, as if that would help clear her confused thoughts. "I don't understand."

"How did Edward feel about your ma?"

"You think Edward—? Oh no, he couldn't have! He loved Mama too much. He wanted to go back to England, too. He always sided with Mama against Papa. He hated this ranch as much as Mama did. He only stayed because of her. He could never have hurt *her*."

"But he could have hurt your pa?"

"No. I don't know. I don't think so."

"He tried to steal that studhorse, Caesar."

"Edward did that?"

Gus nodded. "I saw him at it."

She considered, then said, "Yes, I suppose he could hurt Papa that way. He tried to rob Papa's safe. I almost caught him at it."

"What happened?"

"I saw him. He didn't see me. I hid and made some noise to scare him away before he could finish doing it. Before anyone else could discover him at it. If Papa had ever found out, it would have broken his heart. He had such grand hopes for Edward. Too grand, I suppose. He could never have been the man Papa wanted him to be. He hated the life Papa wanted for him. I suppose he meant to steal enough money to leave the ranch and go back to England. With Mama gone, there was no more reason for him to stay here."

"Only after that your Pa stopped keeping a lot of money in the safe," Gus speculated, "so Edward figured he'd steal the studhorse and sell it for enough to get him where he wanted to go."

Vicky nodded in agreement.

He told her then, "Edward had help stealing the horse."

"Who?" she asked.

"The same man who murdered him."

"Do you know who it was?"

"Eli Tyler."

"Eli! Why would Eli do such a thing?"

"Dora Niles was Eli's sister—"

"What?"

He nodded. "Dora was his sister, and he wanted her to marry rich. He wanted her to marry your pa. He had it planned from the beginning, even before your pa got to know Dora well. Likely he planned it from the time he came to work on the ranch here." Thinking of Eli, Gus wondered where the hell the ranch hands were. Rising, he gestured for Vicky to follow him. He led her into the parlor. Walking to a window, he gazed out as he said, "It was Eli who got your pa and Dora together in the first place. When your ma wouldn't give your pa a divorce, Eli decided to set up evidence for your pa to get the divorce himself."

"Eli put that note in the pterotype machine?"

"Likely he sent notes of some kind to this Rod feller and your ma, too. Notes that would be sure to get the two of them out to the woods, to the same place at he same time. Maybe there never was anything between the two of them at all, but Eli set it up so it would look like there was. And so your pa would see it for himself. Only you got the note before your pa did. Your pa never showed up in the woods. He never had any reason to."

"Then Eli killed Mama and Rod?"

Gus nodded. "He would have gone out there to watch and make sure everything worked the way he planned it. When it didn't, and your pa didn't show up, he got scared. Rod and your ma knew they hadn't sent each other notes. They might tell about it, and your pa might start trying to find out what was going on. That sure as hell would have ruined things for Eli. So he shot the two of them. That solved his problem of getting your ma out of the way. He could figure that after the bodies had been found and the mourning was over, your pa would be free to marry Dora."

"But everyone would have thought Papa killed them —the way I did!"

"That wouldn't matter to Eli. He knew your pa would never be convicted. Likely never even go to trial. All that mattered to Eli was getting your ma out of the way. Only you ruined that for him."

"I did? How?"

"You hid the bodies and nobody found them. Everybody figured your ma had run off with Rod. They all figured she was still alive. Until there was proof she was dead, your pa couldn't remarry," Gus told her. He was still gazing out the window. There was still no sign of the riders. The ache of worry for Dolph was growing in him, drowning his thoughts.

He was aware of Vicky standing close behind him. He sensed the effort it was taking for her to control herself. It was a damned hard thing for her to calmly discuss the murders of her mother and her brother this way. But she needed the truth as badly as he did, and she fought her own fears to find it.

He heard the quaver in her voice as she said, "What about Edward? Why did Eli kill him?"

She was managing to control herself. He thought he should be able to do as well. Concentrating, he forced himself back to the problem, and the solution he had been working out.

He said, "Eli had to get your ma's body found if he could, but he couldn't just go poking around hunting it himself or folks might wonder what he was up to. So he worked out that if he killed Edward and made it look like suicide and left that note saying the bodies were hid, then there'd be a hunt for the bodies, but not for a killer."

She was silent for a long moment. Suddenly she asked, "Do you see anyone?"

He shook his head.

"When they come, Eli will be with them."

"Yes, ma'am."

"Mister Widner, if Eli was planning to kill Edward, why would he help Edward steal Caesar and run away?"

That was a good question. Gus wasn't sure of the answer. But he could make a guess. When he had seen the two men with the studhorse, one had been holding the lead rope. The other was carrying a rifle, but shifted it to his left hand and drew a revolver with his right. At that moment they had realized they were being watched.

He said, "I think Eli wanted to get Edward away from the ranch to do the killing. But I interrupted him before he could finish it, so he had to change his plans. Then Edward got scared that I might recognize him and let on to his pa that it was him up there with the stud-horse. You recollect he did some drinking just after I got here? Likely the more he drank, the scareder he got, until he decided the only safe thing for him was to kill me. But he missed and hit your pa instead. That was—"

He winced suddenly at a sound from the kitchen. His hand went automatically to his hip. But the Leech & Rigdon wasn't there. And he had dropped the pocket pistol when he was struggling with Vicky for the shotgun. For a flick of an instant his empty hand groped. Then it grabbed for a rifle from the wall rack.

Vicky recognized the sound before he did. "The coffee! It's boiling!"

Gus sighed.

"Do you want a cup?" she called to him as she hurried toward the kitchen.

"Yeah," he answered, looking at the gun in his hand. He felt a little foolish throwing down on a pot of coffee. Spooky as hell, he thought. But there was good cause. When the ranch hands got back, there could be some damned tight moments before the trouble was settled. Carrying the gun, he turned to the window again.

There was still no sign of the riders.

18

Gus stood at the window, wondering just how long it had been since he sent the Crow woman to bring back the ranch hands. Not as long as it seemed, he supposed. This kind of waiting was a slow, painful thing. It could drive a man crazy.

Eli Tyler'd had some long waiting while he schemed and maneuvered to get his sister married to a rich man. He had been thwarted again and again. By now he must be tight-strung damned near to the snapping point. Maybe he was already past it. Busting loose and beating up Dolph the way he had done was a senseless thing. A crazy thing. Maybe Eli was crazy.

Behind him Gus heard the opening of a door. Then Vicky's small footsteps. He figured she was bringing the coffee. As he started to turn, he realized there was another sound. The fall of a heavier foot. She wasn't alone.

He swung up the rifle as he turned.

Vicky was coming into the parlor. She moved awkwardly. There was an arm around her throat, choking her, forcing her into each step she took. The muzzle of a revolver was thrust past her side, pointing toward Gus. Eli Tyler was behind her, holding her as a shield.

Grinning, Eli fired.

Gus felt a sudden jolt. He heard the roar of the blast as if it were the sound itself that was slamming into him, spinning him around, sending him sprawling on his belly. The rifle slipped from his hands. A heavy green haze filled his eyes. As he hit the floor, he saw the rifle dimly through the haze. It was in front of him. He wanted it.

He needed it. But when he tried to grab it, his hand refused to move. And then Eli was snatching it up, taking it away from him.

A horrible, sickening feeling of helplessness filled Gus's gut. He realized he couldn't move. The haze pressed in on him. He could see only blurs through it. The sounds he heard were like echoes from some faraway place.

With effort he clung to awareness. He could hear Eli speaking. He struggled to make out the words.

"I had a notion he'd come back here," Eli said. "Damn him, he couldn't do nothing but make trouble."

Appalled, Vicky groaned, "Why?"

Eli heard the accusation in her voice. His answer was a whine of self-pity. "I *had* to do it. You don't know what it's like being damned dirt poor, always grubbing for some damned son of a bitch who's getting rich off your sweat. Then you start getting old and you know it ain't ever gonna be any different. Not unless you do something yourself to make it different. You got to do something quick, before it's too late. There wasn't anything else I could do. I did what I did because there wasn't any other way. I never wanted to kill anybody. I swear I didn't. That old lady of yours made me do it. She wouldn't give in and get the hell out of the way. She wasn't any good. She deserved to die. I *had* to do it, you understand?"

"No," Vicky said. Her voice was all breath and full of fear.

"It's all for your pa's good," Eli told her. "Ma'am, Dora will make him a fine wife. A lot better one than your ma ever did. You'll thank me for it, once him and her are married. Believe me!"

"But she's dead."

"*What!*"

"She's dead. She fell and broke her neck."

"No!" Eli screeched.

"She is," Vicky said softly. "She's dead."

There was silence. A long silence. During it, Gus felt

as if he were fading away. Slipping into a wadding of dark clouds. But he couldn't let that happen.

As he fought to remain conscious, he began to feel pain. It started small, just a lump of pain like a little thing covered with thorns buried in his chest. He could feel it growing, spreading, stretching out spiny arms to fill his body. The spines became spears of flame burning through him, piercing deep into his being.

He thought he could escape the pain. All he had to do was let himself slide into those dark clouds. He could rest there, comfortable and away from the hurting and the worrying. It was tempting. Damned tempting. He might have let himself slip. But just then Eli broke the silence.

Eli spoke to himself, his voice a moan. "I can't lose it all. I worked too damned hard for it."

Then he spoke to Vicky, his words a demand. "I can't let it go! You hear?"

"I hear," she said faintly.

"I ain't a *bad* person. You know that. You know I'm a good man. I never would have killed anybody if they hadn't made me do it." He was half wheedling, half insisting.

In a thin, jagged voice, Vicky said, "Why did you kill Edward?"

"Hell, ma'am, he was no good. Just a damned drunkard. He wasn't any loss to anybody. It didn't matter about me killing him. But you're different, Miss Vicky. You're a handsome woman. A fine woman. I admire you. I don't want to hurt you."

But he would hurt her, Gus thought. He was going to kill her. He had to be stopped.

How?

Gus told himself he had to find a way. He had to pull himself free of the heavy haze that meant to swallow him. Pain or no pain, he had to find the way.

Vicky was fighting her own battle. She was stalling for time. She knew her danger. She was fighting for her life with words.

Struggling against horror, she asked Eli, "Why did you have to kill Gus Widner?"

"He just kept messing things up for me. He was only a damned drifter. He don't matter. But *you* matter, Miss Vicky. I don't want to hurt you. Can't you understand what I mean, ma'am? Can't you see that I *had* to do what I did?" He was pleading, making a desperate demand that she accept what he was saying. Accept it or else.

Gus knew she couldn't stall Eli much longer. She needed help now. To help her, he needed a gun. Vaguely he remembered a gun. A little pocket pistol. He'd had it in his hand a long time ago. He'd dropped it when he fought Vicky for the shotgun. It should be somewhere on the floor. If only he could find it. Reach it. Use it.

He gazed at the blurs in front of his eyes, forcing them to take shape. It hurt, but slowly the shapes became recognizable. He could make out the floor . . . animal-hide rugs . . . the edge of a chair. He managed to twist his head slightly, and saw the hem of a skirt. Vicky was halfway across the room. She was standing between Gus and Eli.

She said to Eli, "I understand."

Eli's tone changed then. Relief and pleasure and hope came into it. "Hell, ma'am, we could get along fine together, you and me. We could do real fine together. You know what I mean?"

Gus saw the pistol. It was under the edge of the chair. It looked a damned long way from his hand.

And Eli was still holding his revolver.

Vicky hesitated. Gus could see that she was trembling. He thought she might faint. But there was steel in her and the troubles she had suffered through were tempering it to a hard strength. She caught a breath, steadying herself, steadying her voice. There was nothing of her terror in it as she said, "You mean you want to marry me?"

"Yes, ma'am!" Eli sounded as happy as if she were accepting his proposal.

He *was* crazy, Gus thought. Pure, outright, hoot-owl crazy. He had to be stopped.

It took effort for Gus to command his body. A damned hell of a lot of effort. Bracing his elbows, he planned his move. It would have to be quick. Only he wasn't sure he could move quickly. He wasn't sure he could move at all against the pain that was surging through him.

But he had to.

Vicky coughed. She gasped and coughed again as she hunted an answer for Eli. Finally she spoke. "I'd—I'd have to ask Papa. I couldn't marry without Papa's permission."

"Sure. Sure enough, honey," Eli grabbed her arm and turned her, starting her toward the staircase. "We'll ask him right now!"

Gus lunged.

Eli saw. And fired. Lead slammed into the floor, sending splinters showering against Gus's outreaching arm.

Gus felt his fingers close over the butt of the pocket pistol. As if in a dream, his mind seemed to stand apart from his body. Distantly he was aware of the motion and the pain. Vaguely he knew his thumb snapped back the hammer of the pistol as his wrist turned the muzzle toward Eli.

With a sudden, startling clarity he saw Eli cocking the revolver again. Saw Eli taking careful aim this time. Saw him squeezing the trigger.

The pocket pistol bucked, flinging itself out of Gus's grip. The world rang with thunder as something hard smashed into his body. It blasted him, shattering him into a thousand dark shards of overwhelming pain.

He had an instant of knowing that Eli was falling.

Of hearing a woman crying.

And then there was nothing.

A woman crying.

A rumble of voices.

Pain.

Darkness.

A sense of having been asleep. Of sleeping like a bear through the winter in a sleep that was close kin to death. A sense of slowly waking.

Gus felt a touch on his face. He heard a voice. It was Dolph's voice, and he wondered whether they were both dead, or both alive. He couldn't be sure. He struggled to find his own voice so that he could ask.

"Brother?" The word whispered through his head. He thought he had managed to speak it.

"You alive, brother?" Dolph asked.

"Are you?"

"Uh huh."

Gus heard himself whisper, "They didn't catch you?"

"They damned near did," Dolph said. "When I kept riding, I rode right slam-bang into that hairpin who went to fetch the deputy. I rode into him and the deputy both together. They saw that I was on one of Boswick's horses, so they stopped me and fetched me back here with a couple of guns pointed at me. We run into Tyler's bunch all right, but they couldn't hardly lynch me with the deputy looking on. Brother, you ain't gonna die, are you?"

Gus forced open his eyes. He could see the fuzzy figures of two people standing in front of him. He seemed to be lying in a bed, and they were at the bedside looking down at him. One was Dolph. The other, with a slender hand resting gently on Dolph's arm, was Vicky Boswick.

They looked nice together, Gus thought. A real handsome pair.

"You've *got* to be all right," Dolph was saying. "Miss Vicky explained about everything, and now it's all straight and we can go home. Ma would never forgive me if I didn't fetch you home in one piece."

"The money?" Gus asked. "You got the money for the mustangs?"

"I talked to Mister Boswick about it. He's in better

shape now than you are, and he says he'll be able to get us the gold by the time you're ready to ride."

"Good," Gus mumbled.

"Another thing, brother," Dolph went on eagerly. "You recollect that filly we bred to the studhorse? We don't have to worry now whether she'll drop us a he-colt. Mister Boswick says he's real grateful for all we did for him and Miss Vicky, and all, and he'd be obliged if we'd accept one of Caesar's colts in appreciation. We'll be able to start a good herd for the family, just like we talked about."

Vicky nudged Dolph. "Tell him the rest."

Suddenly Dolph looked uncomfortable, as if he had bad news.

"Something's wrong?" Gus said.

Vicky smiled.

Dolph shuffled his feet and cleared his throat. "I'm—uh—I'll be going home with you and the money, Gus, but I won't be staying there long. I kinda—well, with Edward and Eli both gone, this here ranch is gonna be shorthanded. Miss Vicky and her pa, they want me to come back here and work for them."

Vicky spoke to Gus then. "If he's as good a cowhand as he says he is, he should be running the ranch in no time."

Dolph's grin was broad and bashful.

He was planning on getting to be more than foreman, Gus thought.

"I'm sorry about leaving you and the family," Dolph said, "but they need me here. You know what I mean, don't you, brother?"

"Sure," Gus muttered. Money and the blooded stud-horse and a place in the world for Dolph with a hell of a lot of promise for the future, he thought. It sounded like the troubles were done and the hard times over at last. Maybe now he could let himself rest for a while.

Smiling, he closed his eyes and sank back into the soft darkness.

Ride into the world of adventure with Ballantine's western novels!

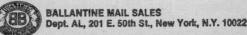